ALSO BY JEAN BOOTH

CHANGED

Library of Congress Cataloging-in-Publication Data Booth, Jean.

Summary: Three months after finding Raif, Natasha is having a
difficult time dealing with her changes. She seeks the assistance of
an ancient vampire for help only to find more secrets.

ISBN-13: 979-8-9893415-2-8

Cover design by: Jean Booth
Printed in the United States of America

For Gail,
Your support, encouragement, and wise words
hidden behind goofy behavior helped me
more than you'll ever know.

JEAN BOOTH

CHANGED

JEAN BOOTH

A morte creou a devastación,
morte será a túa preservación.

Death created devastation;
death shall be your preservation.
-Atlantean Prophecy

1

I was running. The waning crescent moon was my only companion. I knew my tiger's body was not a form I should be in—far too conspicuous—but it was currently my favorite. I liked the playful independence of the tiger, the way this body moved, and the coloring of my pelt. I kept to the depths of the mountain forest to cover my bright orange stripes. I stalked until the call of the open field was too much. There was something about the open fields that seemed to ignite a childlike feeling of contentment. It was a feeling I'd been desperately seeking for weeks. I knew playing in the open field was dangerous, but right now, I didn't care about the consequences.

I would allow myself a few pounces before slinking back into the protection of the surrounding forest. I dug my front paws into the dirt, my rear end high in the air, and eyed the perfect patch of flowers. My feline eyes were level with the tops of the moon-kissed leaves. Twitching the tip of my tail high in the air, I pounced. Petals, pollen, and leaves flew everywhere. I rolled in the patch of displaced flowers, purring and sneezing in delight at the rainfall of petals.

In my own delirium, I almost missed the sound of a gun safety being released. It was the faintest of clicks, yet it caused my movements to stop abruptly. I crouched, allowing the petals and leaves to cover my stripes as I listened for the gun over the thundering of my pulse. This had been a reckless mistake, one that reminded me that I wanted to see tomorrow.

My nose twitched. There was a man with a freshly oiled gun across the field. I figured there had to be at least a hundred yards between us, and if my nose was scenting things correctly, he'd been drinking. Unless he was a sharp shooter, I was positive I could make it to the protection of the forest before he could pull the trigger. I peered over the broken flower stems, ears pinned close to the top of my head. The forest wasn't far, about two body lengths to my right.

All my senses at high alert, I leapt up and ran. I heard his frightened exclamation just before the explosion of the gun. Tree bark splintered a foot from my head, causing me to alter my path. I zigzagged my way deeper into the forest's protection, adrenaline pumping at the thought of how close the bullet had been. Picking up my pace, I gave my animal side free reign. Relying solely on my tiger's natural agility to maneuver through the woods, I wove into the forest, using movements that were becoming second nature. My whiskers received more input than my human brain could catalog. My tail counterbalanced me to keep my body upright and my movements fluid.

Adrenaline pumped through me as I darted through the forest. I knew I'd lost the man, but the excitement of almost being shot and the joy of releasing control to my animal nature kept me running. The thought of being pursued, being hunted, caused me to run faster. My muscles bunched and flexed, heating as I ran.

All too soon, I found myself at the clearing I'd set up for my change. I sat, my sides heaving in an attempt to get enough oxygen. I was exhausted and starving. I refused to hunt in this form, finding the act of physically destroying another life abhorrent. I was certain I'd never completely let go of the humanity that defined me, never fully release control to my animal instincts. The human food was a reward of sorts, congratulating myself on yet another successful change. My breathing began to slow, and I knew what had to happen next. I shuddered, feeling more anxiety over the change than I had over the bullet a foot from my head.

The change hurt. Every time. I listened to the sounds of the forest and attempted to draw some peace from the leaves rustling in the wind. I was tempted, as always, to stay in the stillness of the forest just a little longer. It was always harder for me to become human than it was to become feline. I wondered, again, if this too was normal. I had so many questions; it was past time I sought answers.

I pictured my human form, and the transformation started like usual: with nausea. My stomach rebelled, followed quickly by the rebellion of every other organ and muscle in my body. I tried in vain to relax as my muscles spasmed. My body convulsed, and I found myself on the ground in a writhing mass of fur, bones, and guts. My vision went blurry. I heard my bones cracking and restructuring, muscles straining with the tension of rearranging to fit my new shape. I no longer knew what my natural form was. Did I maintain my humanity? The pain reached a crescendo, and just as I thought I couldn't take anymore, it was over.

Sweat coursed over my naked body, and I began to shiver. Small aftershocks of pain streaked through my veins, causing my muscles to involuntarily twitch. I wanted to close my eyes and give in to the pain and exhaustion, but I knew from experience that I had to eat first. If I waited, I would wake ravenous and end up killing the first thing that crossed my path and eating it raw. The thought caused my stomach to turn. I dressed, the messages from my brain to my limbs taking an excessive amount of time. My whole body felt heavy. My once tight clothes were now loose on my thinner, more muscular frame. I'd changed in so many ways since Atlantis; I was starting to forget who I'd been.

As I opened my backpack, the smell of the three double cheeseburgers inside drifted out, and my stomach growled. It took until I started on the third cold burger to feel somewhat normal. I knew I'd have to stop at a drive-through on my way home, but at least this way I wouldn't hurt anyone. When I got back to the house, Ashlyn would still be in bed, and Katie still at work, so I wasn't too worried. I just wanted sleep now that I'd exerted some of the restless energy I'd had since leaving Atlantis.

Since leaving Raif, my life had become hiding out in the woods to avoid civilization, running at every chance I had. I wasn't certain yet whether I was running toward or away from something, but I knew I couldn't do this blindly anymore. I needed answers about what was happening to me. I had to find someone who could provide guidance, understanding, and most of all, direction. As much as I hated to, I had to go back to the Krypt Keeper and see Stephan.

I gathered my garbage and cleaned my clearing, leaving no trace of my existence. I couldn't be discovered and sent to live the remaining days of my life in a lab. I knew firsthand the life those animals lived and shuddered in sympathy for their captivity. I began the quarter-mile hike down the mountain to where I'd parked my motorcycle. I loved riding almost as much as I loved running. It was the human equivalent, but faster and less reliable than my animal shape. When I ran, I knew instinctively that my feline body would react to protect me from my surroundings. I had no such guarantees when I rode. Instead, I had to put my trust in the machine, and other drivers. The thrill of riding was usually enough to get me through another day. I was so tired tonight though, that the thought of riding back home elicited a groan of frustration.

Even seeing the shiny blue sport bike waiting under the moonlit sky couldn't bring me out of my melancholy mood. I hopped on the bike, revving it to hear the happy purr, and was off. The chilly mountain air bit at my exposed skin, and I embraced it, hoping it would wash Raif's face from my mind. There were more days I wished I'd never gone to Bermuda, never stepped foot on Atlantis, than there were days of joy at what I'd become.

I missed Raif. It was a pain that went bone deep. I wished we'd had more time together, that he could've been the one to show me all the things that were different now that we were mated. I was angry with him for not warning me, for abandoning me when I needed him the most. As angry as I was though, what I wanted most in this world was to be held by him.

I stopped by a 24-hour fast food place on my way home to get something else to eat. I craved protein more than ever since I got back, easily putting away three large steaks at a time and still managing to be hungry. My appetite and change in appearance were at the top of the list of questions I had. I placed the food into my backpack and rode home in relative peace and quiet. Knowing that I had warm food in my bag spurred me to faster than normal speeds.

Katie's light was on when I pulled into the drive. She was home early and waiting for me. I felt a twinge of apprehension at this knowledge, followed quickly by irritation that she was home instead of at work. I just wanted to scarf down my chicken sandwiches and pass out. I snuck into the kitchen, leaving all the lights off, as I didn't need them anyway. My night vision, like so much else, had increased exponentially. Too late, I realized that sneaking in was pointless; Katie had already heard the bike.

"You're home late," she said as she flicked on the light.

I winced and grunted an indecipherable response, hoping she would leave and I could continue to avoid this conversation. I plopped down on one of the kitchen chairs and started eating my sandwiches.

"Tash, please. I think we need to talk. There's been something going on for almost three months, ever since you got back from Bermuda. You've been distant and angry. I know there are things going on that I'll never understand, but you used to talk to me. I want to help." She was pleading, her eyes filling with tears of frustration at my continual avoidance. I had a pang of guilt, quickly extinguished by my hurt and anger.

"When were you going to tell me?" My voice was even rougher than I'd intended as I spoke with bits of bread sticking to my teeth. I'd hoped to avoid this conversation; the pain of her lies hurt almost as much as my changes did.

Surprise was evident in her tear-filled eyes. She clasped her hands in front of her and wouldn't meet mine. She sank into the chair across from me, her legs shaking too much to hold her. The smell of her distress was an aphrodisiac to my carnal nature, although I was relieved to note the sliver of shame at the knowledge that she was afraid of me. I must still have a shred of humanity left after all.

"Tell you what?" she asked, still avoiding my eyes. I almost believed her innocent act, as I had for years. However, there was no hiding or denying it anymore. I knew the depth of her betrayal, knew it the first time I'd changed and scented Ashlyn.

"When were you going to tell me that Keith is Ash's father?" My tone was even, as though I was asking her to pass the salt. I reined in my hurt and temper in a final attempt to allow her to deny the truth, cursing myself at the pang of hope I had that I was mistaken, that somehow my senses had been wrong. The truth had assaulted me the first time I'd changed. Ashlyn's scent had wafted out the door and I knew. The man I'd been engaged to eight years ago was her father.

Katie was silent for a moment. I held my breath and counted my heartbeat four times before she hung her head and sighed.

"I wanted to tell you, so many times." Her shoulders shook in a silent sob. "I didn't know how to say it, and after a while, it just didn't seem important. We'd moved past that. We were happy. I couldn't destroy that."

"How about, 'Tash, I'm the reason your fiancé left you. By the way, we're having a baby?' It's been eight years, Katie; you had time. Instead, you continued to lie and cover it up, pretending it never happened, when the proof of your betrayal is curled up in her bed!" My skin tingled in anticipation of another change. It was always harder to control it when my emotions were high. I took a few calming breaths. She waited for me to continue, knowing I had more to say and accepting my anger. "The weird thing is, I don't even care that you two were together. It might have bothered me in the past, but now I just hope things work out for the two of you, for Ashlyn's sake. What really hurts, what kills me, is that you lied to me. For eight years, you lied. You're my sister, the only family I have. I should be able to trust you completely, without question. How could you do that to me?" Acknowledging her betrayal hurt more than when I'd first discovered the truth. There was a pain in my chest, an ache I'd been trying to avoid that was almost as painful as the loss of Raif. If I still had tears, I'd be crying.

"I'm so sorry, Tash." She looked up at me, tears streaming down her face. She looked so pitiful, so forlorn. Her regret was evident, but I didn't care anymore. She'd broken something in me that could never be repaired.

"Does Keith know that he has a daughter?" I said quietly, her tears deflating me of my righteous anger. Before she could respond, another thought occurred to me. "Alex knew, didn't he? That's why he left."

Her face flushed, breaking my heart even further. I felt guilt at the years of disrespect and anger I had built up toward her ex leaving so suddenly. Now, I understood.

"He figured it out and confronted me. I asked him not to tell you about it. I wanted to tell you myself. Keith didn't even know until three months ago. I knew I had to tell him when I saw you two at the airport. That's where I was when..." she hesitated for a moment, "when you were having your first episode. We thought it best for him to stay away until I could talk to you and figure out what's been going on with you. I've wanted to talk to you about this. I just didn't know where to start. You've had so much to deal with lately; I didn't want to add to it. I'm so sorry, Tasha." We sat in silence, neither one of us knowing where to go from here.

"I hope you do the right thing from now on. Ash and Keith deserve to know each other. You both deserve a chance at happiness. If he can forgive you for hiding his daughter from him for the past eight years, I think you'll be very good for each other." My voice was quiet, firm with resignation. Just because I couldn't forgive her, didn't mean I wanted her to be miserable.

"You're okay with this? You want us to be a family?" The shock and hope in her voice was plainly evident. A bitter smile curved my lips.

"I've always wanted what's best for you, for you to be happy." I sighed, leaning back in my chair as my emotions cooled. "Ash is going to need someone new to torment when I leave anyway."

"Leave? Where are you going?"

"I've needed to talk to you, too. I have to get some help with my...episodes, as you call them. What's happening to me doesn't feel right. I have to find out what's going on. There's someone in Miami that can help me figure everything out. I'm leaving tomorrow and don't know when, or if, I'll be back."

"You're not okay with this. You're just going to run away so you don't have to face it." I was shocked to hear the anger coating her words. "What, you can't get the right drugs here? I know something's been going on. No one can eat that much and lose weight. What is it? Meth? Some new-fangled drug they can only synthesize in Florida? I've trusted you with my kid, hoping you'd snap out of whatever crap you started after you came back." She sat with her arms crossed, tears drying in streaks down her cheeks as she flushed with anger. "Now you're leaving without any explanation. What the hell am I supposed to tell Ashlyn?"

I bristled.

My animal instincts clouded my better judgment, and I started to growl. I allowed my animal nature to surface ever so slightly so that Katie would fully understand why I had to leave. I stood, placing my hands next to her so that she was trapped within the circle of my arms. Leaning into her personal space, my body trembled while suppressing the urge to transform. My other form still didn't understand the complexity of human emotions, and it wanted to protect me from the perceived threat that was my sister. I would never, could never, hurt her, but she didn't know that. I simply wanted to intimidate her, gain her undivided attention. Fear rolled off her in waves. I sensed she was beginning to understand.

"Katie, I have never and will never do drugs. The fact that you thought for one minute I would ever place Ashlyn in danger kills me. I love that kid like my own. I want you to listen carefully." My voice was cold, hard with suppressed rage. "I honestly don't care what you do anymore. You've made it perfectly clear to me how little love and respect you hold for me. I truly want you to be happy, even if that means you create a family with Keith. I need help. I have a problem that no one here is capable of dealing with. I have to figure out what's wrong with me, and I can't do that here." I stalked out of the kitchen and into my room, leaving Katie trembling in her chair. I was done talking. It was time for answers.

2

It'd been three months since I'd left Atlantis and learned that I could change. Three months since I'd discovered everything I believed in, loved, and understood in my life was a lie. I shuddered, suppressing the memories as much as I could, trying to maintain my emotional control. I had eight hours to stay numb before I would be back at Stephan's. He was the only person I could think of that could help me now. The absurdity of the fact that I was now depending on a vampire for assistance was not lost on me.

I curled up in my seat, watching the clouds pass by the airplane's little window, and let the monotony of the view lull me to sleep. The exhaustion of the past couple of days, compounded with the stress of the last few months, finally caught up with me in my dreams.

I fled into my room at Katie's house. My skin was itching painfully. I felt stretched, like I was going to explode in every direction at once and the only thing stopping me was the thin barrier of my skin. A wave of pain hit me so hard and so quickly that I barely made it to the garbage bin before I threw up. I needed to be outside in the fresh air.

The full moon cast shadows in the yard. My stomach clenched again, and I dry-heaved into the rosebushes Katie had planted by the back steps. I heard Ash following me, and I yelled at her to call her mother and stay inside. I didn't know what was wrong with me; all I knew was that I didn't want her to get hurt. The last coherent thought I had was hoping that Ash would listen to me for once.

The images came next. Ashlyn's silhouette in the doorway, searching the yard for me. A glimpse of the stars as I writhed on the ground.

"Aunt Tasha, Mommy isn't answering her phone, and the lady at her work said that she wasn't there tonight. Are you okay? Aunt—" An involuntary growl escaped my throat. *The growl was like a gateway to my animal side. Once it'd been opened, I couldn't gain control of it.*

I let out a deafening roar, my whole body confused but desperate to protect Ashlyn. My niece fell flat on her butt a few feet from me, still unable to see me in the shadows.

The scents of the night assaulted me. Each blade of fresh grass was distinct to my new nose. The wind blew scents off the mountain. In my new form, I could smell things that I had never been able to detect before. Coyotes had been here last night, sniffing out prey. The scent of a rabbit's remains decomposing farther up the mountainside churned my stomach. Both the lioness and I thought it should have been buried better. The lioness...my new form.

Ashlyn was lying before me; the scent she was giving off both excited and confused my lioness. It took a moment to identify the scent, but soon I realized. Ashlyn was afraid of me. My beast and I didn't like that she was afraid of us. I was grateful when the beast I'd become, the beast that seemed to have a mind of her own, decided that Ash was ours and started purring to ease her fear. We slowly crouched forward, inching out of the shadows on our belly to ease Ash's fear and expose ourselves to her.

Ashlyn crawled toward us, reaching out with her palm up. She was muttering to herself, and when I concentrated, I realized she was saying, *"good kitty,"* over and over again. We let out a small snort of frustration. I couldn't talk to her like this. I wanted to explain that this beast was really me, that she was safe. Another part of me knew that it was best that I couldn't explain. I didn't even know what was happening to me, how could she be expected to understand? She touched our nose, and we let out tension I didn't know we were holding in a sigh. Ash giggled as the warm air blew her hair back.

She petted the soft, short hairs on the top of our nose, smiling when we leaned closer to her. My beast listened and scented the area for trouble the entire time Ashlyn was near. That we could

11

multitask so well amazed me. We nudged Ashlyn's body with our head and licked her face as we marked her as our own. We were rewarded with a squeal of delight.

Ashlyn smelled and tasted of a musky cinnamon apple. The musky scent was the exact scent I associated with Keith. The knowledge that the two of them must be related hit me so hard it almost took my breath away.

The sweet apple smell was all Katie. She always smelled pure, sweet, and crisp. It was a smell now forever associated with betrayal. The cinnamon was all Ashlyn. I'd smelled that scent for the past eight years in my human form while we cuddled reading stories at night.

The scenting seemed to calm the animal side of me, and I was able to gain control over my body again. I was still stuck in the form of the lioness, but she was content to let me lead.

I flattened myself against the grass, making myself appear as tame as possible so Ashlyn wouldn't be afraid. She stroked my nose, talking to me like I was her pet. I tried walking, finding that I needed to share responsibility with my animal instinct rather than attempt to control it. Ash knew nothing of my inner battle. She followed me around, chatting and giggling with her new friend. She didn't understand the danger she'd have been in if I was a real lioness.

Ashlyn quickly grew bored of my antics and wandered back into the house. I could hear her pause her video game occasionally and dial the phone. I assumed she was attempting to call her mother or my cell phone.

Suddenly, I was walking into a castle, human again. I knew this castle. It held wonderful memories, ones that I cherished and longed for. I wandered the halls, searching for the lavish gardens that held my love. Instead, I found myself in a chamber I'd never seen before.

It was a cold, bare room, bereft of any loving mementos. Somehow, I knew this was a room meant for cold, clinical calculations—a war room. I crept into the room, aware there was a debate going on. Three people were arguing over something at a small, round, stone table—three people that I remembered from my recent past, one of whom I loved dearly.

"She's not ready. I feel her confusion, her anger...her pain. She's not ready, yet." Raif's face was reddening, pleading with Atreyu to understand.

"Poseidon wants this done now. He knows of your sacrifice, of the prophecy. He is being as patient as a god is able to be. How much longer should I tell him he must wait for you?" Atreyu's bored tone held an edge, warning Raif.

Raif hung his head. "I don't know. I should have told her more, but in truth, I didn't fully know what to expect. I should be with her now. It is killing me to feel her pain and be unable to help her through it. I thought this would be easier with less contact." His voice trailed off as his broad shoulders slumped. He laid his head in his hands on the cold table. I found myself at his side and reached out to comfort him. My hands passed through his defeated form.

"Raifuku, none of us knew what to expect." Cleito was different from when I'd seen her last. She had a hardness to her that surprised me. She was both less and more than what she'd been, and my heart grieved for her. "She is a strong woman; you must trust that she will find a way to cope. You cannot mourn what cannot be changed. We must continue with what must be done. Give her until the Hunter's Moon. I can convince Poseidon to wait until then. After that, you must do what is necessary." Her voice went soft. "If that is still what you wish. We would all understand if things have changed."

"We are no longer alone. Please turn off all electronic devices and place your seat backs and tray tables in their full upright and locked positions." Atreyu looked directly at me as he spoke.

I blinked, opening my eyes to the view of the ocean meeting the sky. It took me a full minute to realize I wasn't in a castle on Atlantis, eight miles below the sea's surface, but actually on a plane preparing to land at the Miami-Dade International airport.

I shook my head, trying to clear out the image of Raif's sweet, concerned face. It hadn't felt like a dream, but rather like an event I wasn't meant to witness. As the clouds gave way fully to the ocean view and the haze of sleep cleared from my brain, the strange dream faded into nothingness.

We landed without issue, and I went to pick up my bags. I had about two hours before nightfall when I would be going to the Krypt Keeper to see Stephan. Forcing thoughts of that meeting from my mind, I focused on what I had to accomplish before I saw him again.

I flagged down a large taxi to take me and the six bags of luggage that contained what remained of my life to the hotel. Three pulled over, and the cabbies all fought over helping me. I was beginning to get used to the unusual amount of attention I got. Ever since the first night I'd changed, it was as though people looked at me differently. It made me uncomfortable still, especially with all the looks I was getting from the other people waiting for taxis.

I picked the first cab and started throwing my bags into the back, not even waiting for him to come to my aid. He grabbed the last bag, struggling to get it into the trunk, and I blushed, realizing that I'd once again forgotten the strength that had come with my change. I hoped no one noticed that I'd pushed all six bags on the tiny cart without any effort or assistance.

The ride to my hotel was strange, yet uneventful. The cabbie kept trying to make conversation with me. He couldn't seem to keep his mind or his eyes on the road. I squirmed in my seat, uncomfortable with his staring and uneasy in the car. I wanted out of the confines of the cab. Enclosed spaces bothered me ever since I returned from Atlantis. Attention from others had always bothered me a great deal.

When we got to the hotel, the cabbie insisted on unloading my bags and seeing to it that the bellboy was as equally attentive to my needs. I checked into my room, unpacked my carry-on, and started getting ready for my reunion. I only unpacked enough so that I could shower and change before seeing Stephan. I couldn't believe how nervous I was. My beast was alert just under the surface of my consciousness, at the ready for any signs of trouble.

I showered, letting the warm spray relax my muscles and wash my apprehension away with the soapy suds. By the time I finished, I was looking forward to seeing Stephan. My beast's anticipation and excitement at seeing someone from Atlantis for the first time was rubbing off on me. As the sun's rays dipped under the horizon, I checked myself out in the large bathroom mirror. Normally I avoided mirrors; the differences in my appearance were nerve-wracking to view. Tonight, though, I looked amazing. I had my black knee-high buckle boots on with tight, black suede leather pants and a blood-red halter top. My breasts were lifted in invitation, something that no longer could be helped with the weight I'd lost. Clothing that fit my breasts now made the rest of me look weird. My hair had turned auburn and hung in loose curls down my back. I felt sexy, powerful, like the predator I now was. Nothing could go wrong when I felt this good.

Walking the block it took to get to the Krypt Keeper, I tried to ignore the whistles and catcalls and just enjoy the muggy heat of Miami in late summer. The Krypt Keeper came into view and my steps faltered. I was unsure of Stephan's reaction, terrified that he'd retract his friendly invitation and I'd be alone again. For the thousandth time, I wished Raif had given me more direction than he had. I squared my shoulders, knowing that even if Stephan did turn me away, I'd disappear from civilization and figure this out on my own.

Thankfully, I didn't have any problems getting into the club and was pleasantly surprised to be directed to a table in the back. I stopped on my way to get some liquid courage. Bolstered with false confidence, I walked to the back tables to meet my fate. I didn't have to wonder what table I should sit at because Victoria was there, waiting for me.

3

Stephan appeared in the room. One minute I was sitting in uncomfortable silence with Victoria, the next his presence hit me like a ton of bricks. My beast rose in me to greet the one that felt like home to us. We could smell him from across the room, like rainwater during a storm. The air around him was charged with power, mixing nicely with the musky cologne he was wearing. I took a deep breath to calm my confusing reaction to his presence, only succeeding in taking in more of his delicious scent.

Victoria gave me a strange look, one that I was starting to get used to by now from her. She shrugged her shoulders in a graceful dismissal of my behavior and stood.

"Stephan." She inclined her head toward him in greeting. Had we been alone, she would have curtsied deeply, showing him the respect he deserved as her master. Since we were in public, she simply bowed her head, tilting ever so slightly at the end to expose her neck in a subservient gesture. "She's acting very strange, even for her. You may wish to tread gently and retire to a less populated area."

I couldn't look at him. Embarrassment had me staring directly at the small of Victoria's back the whole time they interacted, not even caring that she was talking about me as if I wasn't sitting in the booth right next to her. I was having trouble containing my beast. She wanted to fling us into Stephan's arms and rub all over him. She wanted the scent of home on us more than our next breath.

I couldn't allow myself to do that. Not only was it completely, horrifically embarrassing, but it also felt like an utter betrayal to Raif. At my reminder of our mate, my beast calmed. She knew of him, felt his faint life force that lived inside us, but she wasn't as aware of him as I was. She hadn't been a part of me when I was with him.

I faintly heard Stephan dismiss Victoria. I watched as she sauntered away, hips swinging seductively in her miniskirt. He stood quietly at the side of the table, waiting patiently for my acknowledgement. I forced myself to meet his molten eyes. The shock I saw in their swirling depths surprised me.

"I'm really sorry to bother you. I didn't know where else to turn. I need help." My voice came out in a choked whisper. I didn't want to be here. I wanted to be stronger than this. He nodded and folded himself gracefully into the seat across from me.

"Natasha, forgive me. I should have asked this of you before you left last time but was too caught up in my own thoughts. It was careless of me to leave you without any direction. Regardless, you are always welcome here, and I will do my best as the High Priest of Atlantis to help you. I ask you now—who are you mated with?" His eyes held mine. I could feel the power, the influence behind his words. Whether intentional or not, he was very manipulative. I felt the desire to tell him the truth about anything he wished to know, but it was a desire I knew I could ignore. His compelling voice didn't work on me.

"You shouldn't waste your power on me, Stephan. I came here seeking help. Whatever you need from me, just ask. I'm neither embarrassed nor ashamed. I'm mated to Raifuku Iochera, and I'm pissed as hell at him for not telling me a damn thing." I leaned back in the booth, relieved at having said what had been on my mind for months.

"Have you changed yet?" he whispered so softly I could barely hear him over the noise of the pounding music.

"Yes. Quite a few times, actually. That's one of the things I wanted to talk to you about. Can we go somewhere quieter? The music hurts my head."

He nodded, signaling for one of his staff as he did so. A young man was at his side before his hand lowered. He was average height, had sandy brown hair, and light brown eyes, lit with excitement. He barely looked old enough to drink, but with how young Stephan looked, this guy could be thousands of years old and I wouldn't have a clue. He didn't feel like Stephan, though, he felt young, normal. He didn't have the weight of decades past that Stephan and Victoria held on their shoulders.

"Yes sir?" He was eager to do his master's bidding. I wondered briefly if it was because Stephan paid him well, or if it was because he fed off the kid. I let it go, knowing that it was none of my business who Stephan fed off.

"Please bring refreshments to my suite. Also, have someone gather Miss Natasha's things and take them to her suite. Darling, where are your bags?" He never took his eyes from me, and I felt heat rush to my cheeks.

"I wasn't sure of my acceptance here, so I rented a room at the same hotel as last time." He stopped me with a slight nod and told the boy to gather everything from the hotel and bring it back. I pulled my key card out and told young man my room number.

The kid was off and running, glad to be of use. I shrugged, hoping Stephan would explain later. I was curious to know how he lived. Truth be told, I was more curious about his life than I had any right to be, and that bothered me.

He stood and smiled at me, holding his hand out in invitation. I took it, feeling nervous butterflies churning in my stomach and my beast sigh in contentment with finally having a connection to our homeland. We went through the crowd, people parting as we moved. He was as graceful as I remembered, his lithe body swaying seductively to the beat of the music. He led me to what I had assumed was a small janitorial closet by the bathrooms, typing in a code to unlock the door.

It opened, revealing exactly what I would expect in a janitor's closet. Brooms, mops, and buckets lined one wall. A shelf with cleaning supplies lined another, and the third wall held a sink with a large drainage area in the floor. The door closed softly, leaving us in the tiny room with nothing but a swinging light bulb that threw strange shadows around the room.

"Stephan, what are we—" He cut me off with a smirk and a wink. It was as powerful as if he had slugged me in the kidneys. I wanted to jump on him, mark him as my own. The thought certainly didn't come from my human side and had me shaking with its intensity. Thankfully, he turned to the wall with the shelves, did something I couldn't see, and a hidden panel slid aside revealing a stairway behind. The stairs led up and down. Stephan led me upward, still holding my hand. The hidden door slid closed behind us, obliterating the pulsating sounds of the club.

The top of the stairs opened up into an average looking hallway with doors on both sides and one at the very end. We went directly to the door at the end of the hall. He opened it and stood aside, allowing me time to take in the room.

It was magnificent. The walls were painted a deep ocean blue. Silver and black sconces lit every two feet, creating a deep, mysterious feel. He had two plush chairs facing a flat screen television on one wall, two doors leading to what I assumed were a closet and bathroom on the adjacent wall, and across from the chairs was a large, king-sized four poster bed.

He gave me a minute to check it all out before directing me to the chairs. We'd just gotten comfortable when a soft knock sounded on the door, quickly followed by the same young man Stephan had spoken to earlier. He carried a platter with two glasses and two chilled pitchers, both with deep red liquid filled to the brim. I was impressed that he didn't spill anything. I'd have had the plush beige carpets stained crimson by now.

"Your drinks, sir. I brought extra, thinking you'd be more comfortable with privacy. I hope I wasn't too presumptuous. Would you like me to pour the first glass?" He carefully placed the platter on the small round table between us, hand hovering over the first pitcher in anticipation.

"Yes, thank you, John. You may assist Marcy for the rest of the night." Stephan was careful to not look directly at John, so he missed the look of absolute bliss that crossed over his face at this new task. My seemingly endless list of questions continued to grow, causing my head to throb.

"Miss Natasha, your belongings are being retrieved. They'll be deposited into your room, where they'll be waiting when you're finished here. If you need anything, just ask one of us and we'll gladly assist." I met his excited eyes as I thanked him. He looked back at me with eager intensity. He left without another word.

"What's wrong with him?" The whisper left my mouth before I could think to censor myself. Thankfully, John had already closed the door.

"What do you mean?" Stephan replied, sipping his drink delicately.

"He's very excited. No one's ever that eager to do things for other people. It isn't natural." I lifted my legs into my chair, tucking my feet beneath me. I settled into the plush softness, prepared for a long discussion.

"You'll find all my staff more than willing to meet any need you may have at any given time." He drank deeply from his glass, refusing to meet my questioning gaze. Settling down in his chair, he crossed his ankles and changed the subject. Since he changed it to the subject I really wanted to talk about, I let him. "Tell me about what happened in Atlantis. Please." I knew he added the *please* for my benefit. Taking a large gulp of my drink, grateful when I felt the familiar relaxing effects of the Dracula's Vein course through me, I started talking.

I told him almost everything that happened in Atlantis, leaving out only the details of my intimate moments with Raif. He didn't need to know those. It felt good to finally be able to tell someone what happened there, to finally be able to put into words my experiences of the mythical Atlantis. I talked for hours, elaborating on all the minute details of everything I saw, felt, and experienced in his homeland. While I talked, he sat back in his chair, sipping his drink and staring at a blank space on the deep blue wall. I wasn't sure if he was listening or lost in thought, and I didn't care. I wanted—needed—to tell someone about Atlantis, and he was the first person I'd been able to talk to about it.

When I finished, we both sat in silence. I chugged the remaining drink from my glass, thinking of my last day with Raif, my emotions warring between grief, anger, hope, and apathy. I replayed every moment we had together in my head, subconsciously releasing the barriers I didn't know I'd placed to protect me from his essence. I could feel him again. It took me a moment to realize that the anger I'd been feeling wasn't just my own; he was just as angry as I. I took comfort in that small connection to Raif.

I risked a glance at Stephan, who continued to watch the blue walls as if they would answer the riddles of the universe for him. It was a long while before he spoke again, ruining the peace I'd finally settled in. He turned his head, the anger swirling in his magnesium eyes startling me out of my tranquility. Belatedly, I realized he wasn't searching for answers so much as trying to gather his thoughts.

"Raifuku has deceived you." His voice rumbled with the anger of a turbulent sea.

4

I slammed the bathroom door closed behind me, angry that Stephan would accuse Raif of betrayal. I looked in the mirror, anger and frustration causing flecks of teal to swirl in my black eyes. The swirling was yet another one of the many changes I'd experienced since mating. I was angry with Stephan and angry with myself for wanting to ignore the truth of his words. Mostly though, I was angry with Raif for leaving me alone. I slumped against the wall, my anger deflating in frustrated desperation. I missed him so much; all I wanted at this moment were his strong arms around me.

I collected myself and opened the door. Stephan was standing with his arms braced against the frame. His magnesium eyes swirled with anger, his body tightly strung, raw power vibrating off him in waves. Refusing to be intimidated by his aggression, I crossed my arms in a defiant stance and stared right back.

"Explain," I demanded, my beast refusing to show weakness. She didn't like anyone trying to intimidate us, no matter how much he intrigued her. I was grateful for her strength. I just wanted to cry or scream in frustration. He sighed, head drooping to his chest with exasperation.

"I do not even know where to begin." His voice was a strained whisper, like he'd been screaming for hours.

"How about the beginning, and we'll go from there?"

"Come." He held out his hand to me in invitation. "You know most of our history, but not our culture. We will start there."

Instead of bristling at his order, I followed him back to the chairs. I was exhausted from the emotional turmoil of the day; my constant inner battle with my beast had drained all the fight out of me. I was dying to know more about the culture of the people I now obviously belonged to, and my beast was dying to be closer to Stephan. Going with him to discover how and why Raif lied was in both our best interests. I curled back in my chair and waited for him to start talking. I didn't have to wait long.

"Atlantis has always been known as the land of the seven isles, ruled by Poseidon. When he had children, he gifted them each portions of the land he loved so much. Atlas was given title of king, and his nine brothers were to be princes of the remaining parts of the islands," he began. "What was purposely kept from the tales was that each clan on each island holds certain powers. As you already know, Raifuku's clan holds the ability to shift shape." His eyes grew dark, the magnesium swirling again in agitation at having to mention my mate's name.

"Yeah. Apparently, we can become big cats. I've already been a lioness, tiger, cheetah, and a leopard." I smiled at him in reassurance that I wasn't unhappy about this development. I loved that I had the power to change; I just wished I'd had some warning beforehand. He softened, relaxing into his chair.

"I'm not surprised that you're coping so well on your own. You're a strong woman. I am surprised at how quickly you've adapted to taking multiple shapes. That usually takes a few decades of intense training to learn." He smiled back at me, finally relaxing as he started his teaching. "Sumner is the isle of the Changers. On the northeastern border, Prince Eraemon ruled. He died with many of the others during the last war. His people are confined to shift only to the shape of a bear. They can take any type of bear form but have never fully been able to embrace any other creature. This shape helps them maneuver across the rocky, mountainous terrain of our homeland. The claws help to grip the mountainsides; their hides protect them in the harsh winters the peaks see almost year-round.

"Prince Autochthon's people are what you know as Werewolves, and they lived in the northwestern portion of Sumner. That part of the island is thick with forest. Wolves are naturally superior in the hunt and protection of that territory. They are pack animals, striving to protect and care for their own above all else." The air chilled, Stephan's eyes darkening as he continued.

"Prince Mneseus ruled the southern border of Sumner, and his people are true Changers. Mneseus was the Warrior Chieftain—a fierce, noble man who valued few things over the passion he held for war. He preferred the agility, stealth, cunning, and independent nature of the cat, but was able to shift into any shape necessary to fight his enemy. Before he died, Raifuku's father was worshiped as a god in many of the lost cultures of the Americas. He went mad, yet hid his slide into madness behind his proud stature. Many died that didn't have to when he was finally destroyed."

"Wait," I said, ignoring the haunted look he held at the memories I was forcing him to relive. "You mean I can shift into anything I want? I'm not stuck as a cat? Not that I'm complaining, but that's incredible." My mind was whirling with the possibilities. I could be a bird. I'd always dreamed of being able to fly, to conquer my fear of heights by changing into a bird and flying to a safer place. My lips curved into an excited grin. Stephan smiled with me.

"Yes, with time you could shift from shape to shape with minimal effort. There have been some who have honed their ability so well that they are able to shift only parts of their bodies, a partial shift. I've been told that it takes extreme power, skill, patience, and energy to shift only a portion of your body. There is even a story of a chimera roaming the lands before it was shot down, leaving only the corpse of a man lying dead in its stead. There was only one being powerful enough to contain the shapes of many, and they say that attributed to his madness."

I sat in horror at the thought of shifting into various parts of creatures and possibly getting stuck like that. I worried every time my body changed that I'd never be human again. A shudder slithered through me as I realized the chimera he was talking about was Raif's father. Thinking back again on my time with Raif, I remembered that he'd walked in the dark, with only his eyes shifted to that of an animal. I knew then that he was powerful, but I didn't truly understand the magnitude of his power until now. I was amazed and humbled at the knowledge that such a formidable person was my mate.

"The royal house, descendants of King Atlas, are telekinetic, as you learned from your human-turned-Atlantean friend, Michael. They can teleport themselves or any object from one point to another. I have heard that King Nereus never honed his powers, preferring to let others do things for him. He shuns his birthright and disgraces the Atlantean way of life." His face contorted in disgust.

"That sounds like a crappy talent for the highest-ranking member of your people," I blurted out, without thinking. I blushed, opening my mouth to apologize. He stopped me with a smirk and slight shake of his head.

"All the powers we were gifted came from the land with Poseidon's blessing. King Nereus had never had to face anything more difficult than deciding what he'd have for dinner, until you came along. I've been told he let his powers wane until they were no stronger than when he'd first developed them. Imagine though, fighting a battle and being able to transport your enemy's army anywhere you wanted in the blink of an eye. It is truly an awesome power in the wrong hands." His eyes glittered with mischief.

I was sufficiently humbled, amazed that any one person could become so powerful. My ability to shift form seemed dull in comparison. I was having a difficult time wrapping my mind around all the implications of what the people of Atlantis could actually do, so I took a sip from my refilled glass to calm my shaking nerves. It didn't help, because he continued.

"Atlas's twin, Eumelus, now controls Melic. That island holds sway on powerful soul magic. Prince Eumelus rules the western borders, which is mostly mountainous with the fertile plane in the south. He leads the Necromancer clan. The ability to raise and control the dead is truly a terrible power to be harnessed. Only those who are pure of heart and strong in mind and spirit are able to truly master and wield this ability.

"Before we sank, Melic was divided between two princes, Prince Eumelus, who we have just discussed, and Prince Amphres. Prince Amphres ruled the eastern half of Melic, a land covered in mountains, its people widely dispersed among the caves and valleys. Prince Amphres learned to communicate with his clan by

Dream-Walking. They have the ability to not only enter another's dreams, but to also shape them into anything they desire. Few, like Prince Amphres, have been so powerful that they've been able to actually transport their dream selves into the reality of another and observe things as they happen."

I shuddered, briefly remembering the strange dream I had on the plane. I was afraid that I may have Dream-Walked, but couldn't bring myself to ask Stephan about it. I wasn't convinced I wanted to hear the answer.

"What happened to him? Did he die when Atlantis sank?"

"Sadly, Amphres went mad after Atlantis sank. We were driven to horrific ends, and he wasn't capable of sustaining life in that manner. He was one of my many brothers who requested a swift execution." Stephan's voice was soft, filled with a pain I hoped I would never know. Clearing his throat, he continued. "I've already told you of the Changers on Sumner. We'll spend the next few weeks getting you comfortable with your animal nature before training you on battle techniques and testing your limitations."

I was a little drunk off the Vein and so excited about the thought of finally learning about myself, I almost missed what came next.

"The last four lands that create Atlantis are centered directly on the compass points. The Elementals, as we call them, all gain their powers from the various elements. The Earthens are stronger on land, Nymphs in the water, and so forth. They can take their element and mold it to their will. Rotsem is in the north. It's a thick, lush, tropical, forested land, and its people control the element of Earth. You want a mountain? The Earthen clan can pull the land forth until the sun is blotted out.

"Prince Elasippus led the Earthen clan until he was killed in a silent uprising about six millennia ago. You were lucky to have met Stuart on the water where his powers were weakest. We'd not be talking now if he'd found you on land." I shuddered at the memory. I still had nightmares of Stuart attacking me on the cruise ship. As disgusted as I was with his demise, I'd be forever grateful to Victoria for killing him.

"To the east lies Horindu, a dry, volcanic land ruled once by Prince Mestor. His people are Pyrokinetic, and they have sway over fire. Diampri is the southern isle, hosting the last of the fertile plane along with the Aeris. Diaprepes once ruled this land, his people controlling the winds that benefit all of Atlantis. Azaes rules the last land, Azazeil. It's found in the west and is a forested land with a naturally occurring spring in its very center. Azaes rules the Nymphs, and they are masters of water. All of Poseidon's kin can control water to some extent, but none are as powerful as the Nymphs. Their mastery is truly something to be admired." He stopped, letting me take in all the unbelievable information he'd given me.

"It's a wonder you were ever defeated," I whispered.

"Arrogance breeds stupidity. We were naïve, drunk on the power we were just starting to accumulate and understand. Atlas thought we should be treated like gods since we held their power. He was a fool! With great power comes great responsibility." He smiled, dimples making a rare appearance. I grinned back.

"What clan do you belong to?"

He beamed at me, and my heart did a little flip that I desperately tried to ignore. "I knew there was a reason I liked you. My brother, Atreyu, and I were born of the mated pair, Horace of the Pyrokinetic clan, and Dina of the Nymph. We were sent into the priesthood of our own free will when were very young. Priests cannot belong to any one clan. They must be males born of two clans and denounce lineage to any. Priests become Atlantis, dedicating themselves first and foremost to Poseidon's will and the desire of the land. We are the keepers of the faith, guardians of the knowledge, and protectors of the fountains. We know all of Atlantis, and because of that, we learn all powerbases.

"When Atreyu and I joined the order, there was only one other apprentice. There have never been more than three apprentice priests and one High Priest living in Atlantis. When our High Priest died, it was up to Percival, Atreyu, and me to choose the next High Priest. I was chosen, and it was I who led the troops on our fated plunder. Since I have been banished to live amongst the Surface Dwellers, and Percival is dead by Poseidon's hand from before we sank, Atreyu is now the High Priest in Atlantis. It is the first time in our history that there are two who could be called High Priest without an apprentice to be found." He sipped his drink, his thoughts lost in the continent below the sea. I had thought I'd come here and have all my questions answered. Instead, I found myself wanting to know more and amazed and slightly overwhelmed with what I'd already learned.

"So, you're the most powerful being on the planet then?" I asked. He smiled and nodded. "And you own a bar?" My eyebrow curled up in confusion, causing him to chuckle.

"My dear, those of us who remain from the original tragedy, that have not succumbed to the madness, have created safe havens for others like us. There are other humans, like you and Victoria, who possess traits of Atlantean descendants and can be converted fully or mated."

"What do you mean?"

"We have lived for thousands of years, Natasha. We've been mating with humans and evolving into something I don't believe we were ever meant to be. I am now vampire, forced to live on the blood of others and able to transform humans into the abomination I've become. They would not have the powers I hold, but they would be similar to the creatures in stories you've read.

"When we mated with the humans, occasionally those couplings created offspring that shared our talents. Most we left to be raised in human society as their talents were mild—muted with your inferior human code." I growled. "My apologies, but it is the truth. Your species is weak and inferior to ours. If it weren't for our strict rules and desire to live amongst you, we would have wiped you from the planet centuries ago. And while you are an inferior species, your genetic code is dominant, hiding most of the traits that would label you as Atlantean. The few who held promise, we monitored until they either faded or the code disappeared from procreation."

"Sometimes anomalies skip generations. You must have had quite a few issues pop up over the millennia," I observed.

"You are right. Victoria was one of those anomalies. She was found by her maker four centuries ago, covered in the ash of her father's barn, not a scratch or burn on her when she should have burned with her family, and no knowledge of what had happened. Her maker knew she was the product of a Pyro who had mated with a human, and converted her to vampire, a thing that was completely unnecessary. He was just entering his madness and turned her without consent. She was his prisoner for the first hundred years of her vampire life. When I destroyed her maker, I found her, along with a handful of others, chained in his basement.

"Some had to be destroyed, having been driven mad by the years of torture. Victoria had been with him the longest and amazed me with her strength of mind. I sent the ones who could be saved to be trained by leaders of their rightful clan, or a clan that was similar, and took Victoria for my own.

"In this bar, our safe haven, we can talk openly about what we are without fear of repercussion. Here, those who fear us, those who fear change, cannot hunt us." His face grew dark and imposing.

"Hunt?" I asked, knowing already that there were those that abhorred change—who would go to any lengths to prevent it. I shuddered again at the memory of my encounter with Stuart.

"Certainly, in all the tales you've heard about vampires, you've also heard of the vampire hunter?"

5

Vampires, Changers, necromancers, and hunters—it was all just so unbelievable. If Stephan had told me any of this three months ago, I'd have laughed in his face. Now that I'd changed, this world didn't seem so unlikely.

I lay in yet another lavish room, the last door on the right before Stephan's, and contemplated everything we'd discussed. Tomorrow, he planned on teaching me about Changers. He'd promised to teach me, first and foremost, how to become one with my animal nature. It was an intimidating thought—to be trained by the most powerful being on earth. With all the events of the past few days swirling in my head, the floral canopy covering my bed eventually became a distraction that my eyes couldn't handle anymore. I closed them, thinking it would be easier to follow my racing thoughts without the distraction of the ugly canopy top, and promptly fell asleep.

The smell of Cleito's garden filled my nose. Raif was sitting on the fountain's bench, his head cradled in his hands. I walked toward him, my feet not making a sound on the soft grass. I didn't want to disturb him, or interrupt the dream as I had last time. I wanted to hold him, to comfort him, and to be comforted in return. Every cell in my body hummed with the need to be in Raif's arms. He looked up, his teal eyes staring straight into mine.

"Raif," I whispered, pain and desire making my voice thick. I was frustrated with the knowledge that he couldn't hear or see me, but the way he started intently at the exact spot I was standing sent hope racing through my veins.

"Natasha?" he whispered back. "Amada, I feel you." Amazement coated his voice, an echo to the feelings I had at knowing he felt me there. He blinked and twin tears fell 'from his eyes. My heart broke at his naked vulnerability. "I can't see or

hear you, but Atreyu thought you'd be back. He told me I'd just have to open myself to you, and I'd know when you were there. I still cannot believe he was right. I hope you can hear me. We haven't had a Walker in our midst for a very long time, and Atreyu was uncertain as to what to expect with you. Amada, *I'm so sorry." His voice broke. "I never knew it would be like this, I swear." His voice was so full of pain and regret; soft and thick as it was, I could barely hear him. He placed his head back in his hands, shoulders shaking as he wept.*

I closed the gap between us, kneeled at his feet, and rubbed his hair. I prayed with everything I had in me that somehow, he could feel me and be comforted. I could feel the soft strands of his hair beneath my fingers, the resistance as my hand met his scalp, and the soft pressure as the strands flowed beneath my fingertips. He slowly looked up as my hand stroked down the long strands. His eyes swam with tears as he looked directly at me.

"Natasha?"

"I'm here. It's okay. I love you. I'm not upset about what happened. I understand why you had to stay. What's happening is bigger than the two of us. I'll be fine until we're together again. I love you." I knew he couldn't hear me; I spoke more to comfort myself. He smiled; the tears he was restraining released with the movement of his cheeks.

"It's true." His voice held such awe. "I can feel your touch. I can even see your shimmer. You are so beautiful, even as a shade. Oh Amada, *do you know what a treasure this is?" I nodded. I knew what a treasure it was to me to be able to see him; it calmed my soul. I could only assume he felt the same.*

"Can you hear me?" I asked, hope echoing from my heart and shattering as he shook his head.

"I can't hear you, my love, I can only see you. It's enough, though, that I am able to look upon you for a moment. You need to know that I love you. I always will." I returned his smile. Mine less haunted, I hoped.

"I," I said as I pointed to my eye. "Love." I made a heart with my hands. "You," I finished, pointing to him. The smile I was rewarded with was worth feeling like a total besotted idiot. We sat,

*grinning like lovesick fools, for an eternity, content just to be close
to one another for the first time in months. It didn't matter that I
wasn't physically there; we could see one another, feel the other's
touch. It was enough. I could have stayed locked like that forever. I
didn't care that it was only a dream, until he started frowning.*

"You're fading," *he whispered.* "I hope you've found
someone to train with, someone who can teach you the things I
cannot. I'm sorry it couldn't be me. I honestly thought it would be
better this way, that it wouldn't hurt as much. Please find
happiness in this life. All I want—"

He disappeared suddenly. Everything disappeared. One
second, we were sitting in a lavish garden, the next: nothing. I was
kneeling in a black void. I couldn't even see the hand I waved in
front of my face, or feel the currents of air I knew it should be
displacing as I waved it back and forth.

"Hello?" I called, my voice echoing and muted at the same
time. I could hear other muted voices but couldn't see or
understand anything they were saying. I couldn't even tell how
close they were, or if they were dangerous. I could feel my heart
thudding in my chest as I strained my eyes to see something—
anything—in the darkness.

I didn't know how I'd ended up in this place, or even where it
was. I had the desire to run, but was frozen, crouched on my knees
as I had been with Raif. Closing my eyes didn't help; it was just as
dark as when they were open. I felt as if there were things all
around, not quite living, but not quite dead.

I wrapped my arms around my body, cursing myself and
desperately wishing I could wake up. A keening noise started in the
back of my throat, and I tried to stop the scream I could feel trying
to escape. Through the muted, echoing noises, I could hear a faint
voice.

"Tasha? Tasha. Follow me. Hear my voice. Dear Poseidon, let
her hear me! Tasha!" The familiar voice paused, waiting. A few
curses sprang forth from his lips; then he paused again. I could
visualize him gathering his thoughts before resuming his chant. I
leapt from my crouch, running blindly toward the voice, ignoring

all the other noises that were starting to grow in intensity and volume.

"Stephan?" My eyes flew open. His magnesium irises were inches from my face, concern pouring off him in waves.

"Thank Poseidon!" His arms wrapped around me, crushing me against his chest, his heart thundering beneath the thin cotton of his shirt.

"What happened? What are you doing here?" My voice rasped against his firm chest, overused as if I'd been screaming for a very long time.

"How long have you been Dream-Walking? Did you even know what you were doing?" His voice held anger, concern, and a hint of fear, all mixed with awe. I knew he felt my shrug yet didn't release me from his embrace. "You, my darling, must be one of the most powerful Dream-Walkers I've ever encountered. It explains how you were able to find Atlantis and why you're such a strong Changer. John came to get me when you started screaming and he couldn't wake you. Has this happened before?" He leaned away from me, placing my shoulders firmly back against my pillows, relief etched on the planes of his face. His excitement at discovering I had another ability almost masked the tightness of his muscles, but I could smell his concern permeating the room. His muscles were slowly relaxing now that I was awake and talking.

I noticed John in the corner of the room. His face was as white as the sheet he was clutching in his hands. He had a tentative grin on his face. He, too, was trying to hide his stress from me. Something bad must have almost happened for them to be so afraid. I tried to ignore the delicious smell of fear they were so desperately trying to cover.

"Thanks, John. I don't quite know where I was for a minute there." My voice was still scratchy and soft. I cleared it as I smiled at him, hoping to further ease his tension before turning back to Stephan. "I used to have strange dreams as a kid that would seem real, but I could never quite remember them until later when I would have a strong case of déjà vu. I always ignored them, and eventually, they went away. When I was flying in yesterday, I had another strange dream. I can't really remember it, but I remember that it was unlike any dream I've had before. Just now, though, I was in Cleito's garden with Raif." Stephan's molten eyes raged at the mention of Raif's name. "You know, you don't have to be such a jerk. He hurts just as badly as I do. He could feel me while I was there! He talked to me—begged for my forgiveness. He and I both know I'm not a delicate flower to be broken by the things I've encountered. So, I think it's time you tell me what it is that you two are keeping from me." He tried to turn away from me, but I took his face in my hands. My head spun with the effort it took to lean forward. I ignored it.

"No! You've told me so much already, and I think I deserve to hear the rest. Spill it." I fell back against my pillows, arms crossed in frustration. I felt awful. My entire body was weak and sore. I didn't understand why I felt so miserable, but I'd be damned if I asked him that before I found out the secret he didn't want to tell me. He glared back at me, testing my resolve. Our gazes were locked in silent battle until he finally relented. His whole body slumped in defeat. I saw a brief burst of pain cross his eyes a second before he turned his head away from me. His voice was tight when he finally spoke.

"It should not be my place to speak of this to you." Anger crept into his tone but never reached his eyes as he continued, "I will tell you, but now is not the time. Give me this next month to teach you what is necessary for your survival, and I will tell you what Raifuku should have told you before you agreed to mating. You have my word that on the night of the Hunter's Moon, I will tell you." He looked back at me, unable to completely hide the pain under his mask of indifference. I nodded. It was the whispered, pain-filled voice that had me agreeing to his terms, not the words. "Now, perhaps we should eat. You look so pale I'm uncertain how you're still able to sit upright." I allowed him to change the subject, mostly because I really was starving. He turned to John, who was so quiet I'd forgotten he was even there. "Please bring something full of protein for our guest and the usual for me."

John scampered out of the room, leaving me with an ancient vampire sitting on my bed. I felt my face redden at the thought of what could happen if we were free to explore the undercurrents of tension between us. I remembered the stolen bite when we first met and felt my entire body join my face in a flush. He turned back to me, his silver eyes crinkled slightly, almost as if he was amused by my wandering mind. I had a horrible thought.

"Please tell me you can't read minds," I whispered. It was his turn to blush.

"Not all are able, but those who have honed the talent can pick a stray vibration, thought, or feeling from others. It isn't so much reading your thoughts as being highly perceptive. Scents alter with each emotion. There are small vibrations and color changes that can alert one to certain thoughts. If you were around your mate longer than you were able to be, you'd have been able to project thoughts just as you do emotions. It's like you're hearing what they're thinking; you're so in tune with each other. I cannot believe you're a Walker." His change of subject was abrupt, but the awe in his voice was intriguing.

"Why?"

"When the islands sank there were few survivors from Melic. Dream-Walking is truly a rare gift. Those who possess it have an easier time with telepathy. Dream-Walking is performed by using mental pathways that are still mostly undiscovered by the scientists of today; we'd always just accepted the fact that it could be done, not worried at the hows or whys of it. As you age and fine-tune this ability, you'll discover variations of ways it can be used. You must be careful though. The Dream-Walkers of old spoke of the thrill of experiences they had achieved while Walking. The incessant desire to know everything, coupled with the actual ability to achieve that knowledge through the dreams of others is heady. During our training, the elders stressed upon Atreyu and myself to beware the Void." I shuddered involuntarily.

"What's the Void?" I whispered. I wanted to be able to see Raif without having to worry about being sucked into that vacuum of nothingness again.

"No one was ever certain what it was exactly. We only know that of those who entered, few ever returned. The pull it has on a Walker is akin to the need I have for blood. Yet, it's a place of death. Many Walkers of the past became lost in the Void, leaving soulless empty shells of people at home. Eventually, the body died, but we have no idea what happens to the lost souls. It's very important for you to only Dream-Walk when I'm with you. I can help you travel and return before you reach the Void." His hand was caressing mine absentmindedly giving me comfort against the terror of his words.

I could have told him what happens to the lost souls. They're trapped forever in the emptiness, calling out to others who enter after them. I was afraid to tell him I knew, that I'd been to the void and returned. I kept shocking him with my abilities, I wasn't certain either one of us could handle another shock.

We were interrupted by a soft knock on the door followed by John entering with the most delicious breakfast I'd ever smelled. My beast rose with the succulent scents wafting toward us. I salivated, growling in anticipation. Stephan grinned at me.

"I see it's been a while since you were fed properly. That changes now. As a Changer your body needs more protein. The more you eat, the less likely you will change at inopportune times."

I was barely paying attention to his lecture. All thought of conversation left with the introduction of those delicious smells. There was a platter of eggs, bacon, and half a honey baked ham, glazed to perfection. There was enough food to feed four healthy men, and I could have eaten it all. Stephan took the tray from John and chuckled as he placed it on my lap.

"Enjoy, *miña mascota*." He raised his goblet to me in salutation and together, we ate.

6

Two hours later, I was clean, stuffed, and waiting by the bar for Stephan to teach me all about changing. It was almost dark, seeing as I'd slept the night and most of the day away. While I waited, my mind wandered to the man I was waiting for. Stephan didn't seem like any vampire I'd read about; he seemed almost normal. His manner of speaking sometimes reverted to a time before now, a subtle reminder to me that he'd been alive for centuries. To anyone who didn't know, his manner of speaking was just an endearing quirk.

A sudden image of Victoria on the boat when we went diving came to me. She'd been covered by layers of fabric that effectively hid her from the sun. I wondered if Stephan would have more or fewer limitations than Victoria since he was so much older than her. I wondered if being a pure-blooded Atlantean made any difference from the vampires who are created.

I closed my eyes and tried to clear my head before my first lesson. I breathed deeply, meditating on my beast's anticipation.

"Calming yourself before the hunt, *miña mascota?*" Stephan whispered behind me. I jumped and, much to my embarrassment, squealed. He chuckled in response, his hand finding mine easily, leading me out of the club to his car.

He had a sleek silver convertible that matched his eyes perfectly. The top was down, revealing a beige leather interior that still smelled new. He held the door open for me as I slid into the soft bucket seats. I practically purred with contentment. I love convertibles.

He slid into the driver's seat and sped off into the Miami traffic toward the Everglades. The roads were completely dark by the time we reached the glades, civilization lost miles ago with the setting sun. My beast and I were in heaven. The sounds and smells intrigued our senses, and the wind whipped my hair into a tornado of tangles. My laughter rang out, the only sound of humanity next to the purr of the engine.

He pulled off onto a small dirt road that was almost completely hidden by the foliage. The road twisted, winding almost upon itself at various times, the branches of the trees missing the car by inches. When we finally pulled to a stop, I could only gape at the scene in front of me.

Ivy scaled the grand old house in front of us. The white paint had peeled back in spots from years of neglect, and the hurricane shutters flopped haphazardly about the windows. The broad, round pillars were faded in misery. I felt a chill run down my spine at the ancient atmosphere in this small clearing.

"What is this place?" I whispered, unable to tear my gaze from the beauty before me. Moonlight filtered through the branches surrounding us, giving the mansion an eerie glow. Crickets and frogs chirped their nightly songs around the corner where I could barely make out a pond. I could smell the pungent water through the misty night air. It was heaven.

"This is my home. It was the first place I lived when arriving to this land. I have updated it since then, but I fear I've not been here for quite some time." He paused. "It's past time it's been cleaned out and lived in again. I own the hundred acres surrounding this lot, so we can run and hunt in relative privacy."

He took my hand, leading me up to the rickety old porch and in through the massive front doors. My mind was whirring at the history the house hid in its bones, the secrets it could tell if one looked hard enough. He stood silent as a statue next to me.

I entered the foyer, blinking to allow my eyes to adjust to the lack of light. I could feel miniscule changes happening to my eyes, changes that allowed me to see better in the dark. When I was finally able to focus, I let out a soft gasp.

Everything was covered in a thick layer of dust and cobwebs. The grand staircase swept up, curving into a balcony that looked over us. The chandelier centered in the ceiling held melted taper candles. The wax congealed in strips from each of the tapers' holders. Simple sconces with melted wax surrounded the room. If lit, they would better illuminate artwork, delicate bric-a-brac, and vast entryways leading off from the foyer. The dark oak doors were all partially closed. It seemed as if someone had left in a hurry without looking back.

I wondered why it was left in such disarray. It didn't fit what I knew of Stephan. I looked back at him. He was framed in the doorway; a breeze ruffled his hair, and the scent of his distress hit me.

On impulse, I wrapped my arms around his torso, holding him tightly to me in an attempt to ease his pain. I had a feeling he rarely, if ever, asked for comfort from people, so I offered it freely.

He was tense at first, either shocked at my show of affection, or unable to accept the comfort I was offering. Slowly, I felt him relax in my embrace, eventually wrapping his arms around me in return. We stood there, holding each other in the doorway in an ancient mansion, listening to the sounds of life all around us. It was peaceful to us both, and a bit confusing. I released my hold on him and started to pull back. He tensed, unwilling to let me go. My heart beat faster.

"Thank you, *miña mascota*. You have no idea what a gift you are to me. Raifuku is a fool. Forgive me, but I am grateful for that." He leaned down and kissed my forehead, turned, and walked out the door. It took me a minute to calm my racing heart. I told myself that my erratic pulse was due to his belittlement of Raif, nothing more. I was unwilling to examine it any closer than that. When I was more in control of myself, I followed him, hopeful to start my training.

I found him in the backyard, staring at the large, murky pond. The glare of the moon was bright here where the trees were sparse. It was like stepping outside at noon after being in a dark theatre for hours. I blinked, attempting to adjust to the brightness, but Stephan put a hand on my arm to stop me.

"Tasha, wait." He used his free hand to trace the curves of my face, successfully freezing me in place. "Open your eyes," he whispered. They flew open, instinctively searching for his expressive magnesium ones. I hoped he couldn't read me as well as I could him. I was devoid of breath, my heart pounding in my chest at his simple caress. Regret, dismay, and confusion warred within me. I shouldn't feel this way about another man. I never thought I would. Raif was everything to me, yet Stephan's fingers on my cheek succeeded at sparking a fire that burned deeper than any I'd ever felt. I blamed the beast. It had to be her; I knew I loved Raif.

"It's not possible. You're too young and still untrained." The awe was evident in his husky voice and in his expression. His eyes roamed about my face. For an ancient vampire, he sure had a hard time schooling his features.

"What? What's wrong?" My voice sounded raspy and thick to my ears. The words were difficult to form.

"You've partially changed. Your eyes and most of your features are feline. How? Have you done this before?" He now had both hands cradling my face, turning it to examine it from all angles. I shrugged my shoulders. I had no idea that I'd changed, let alone whether I'd ever done it before.

"I don't know. I don't think so. Usually, the change is painful. This was easy. I wanted to see, knew I could, so I did. It's hard to talk." My jaw hurt. Words weren't meant to be formed with a jaw that was shaped like mine. My voice sounded strange to my ears. He smiled.

"Perhaps you don't need my help after all." He looked at me for a minute more before releasing my face. "You said it's usually painful to change. Why?"

"Seriously? My bones break and reform. It's not exactly a party."

He laughed, transforming his face into that of an angel—an angel with sharp, pointy teeth, but an angel nevertheless. My beast was alert—craving him, wanting to see what other expressions she could elicit. I was appalled by her desire, knowing that my husband, my soul mate, should be the only one igniting that type of response from either of us. I pushed her down as far as I was able.

"I understand the mechanics of what happens to the body during the transformation. It is uncomfortable, certainly, but should never be painful. I'm amazed at how you've been able to grasp the most advanced form of changing, when you don't even know the basics." He sighed and shook his head. "Rule number one is more of an understanding and acceptance than an actual rule. You and the beast are one and the same. There isn't another creature, life force, entity, whatever you want to call it, living in you. It's you, just another facet of your personality. Once you accept that, changing your forms will be no more difficult than changing clothing. It does require more protein than changing clothing, but you understand my meaning."

"No! She's different from me. I feel her desires separate from mine." I couldn't accept that the beast was really me. If I did, then I'd have to accept everything that came with that. Her carnal nature, the thrill of the hunt, and the way she craved Stephan—it wasn't me! It couldn't be me. Mistaking my denial for disgust, his face softened.

"I know how hard it is to accept the need and desire to hunt. It goes against your human nature. But the sooner you stop treating your animal nature as different, the easier the changes will become. Once you accept it, embrace it, you will find peace. Now, let's see where you're at. Let's run." His eyes sparkled in mischief seconds before he changed into a famed Florida panther.

I stood dumbstruck for a full minute. I'd forgotten he was a priest and could change. Once I'd gathered myself, I held up my hand, telling him to wait, and walked around the corner of the house for privacy. This was going to be fun.

I stripped off all my clothing, leaving it in a neat pile in the shadows of the house. I thought about how quickly Stephan changed; his clothes had just vanished. I then focused my thoughts on the creature I wanted to become, bringing my beast closer to the surface, giving her permission to take over. I grunted with the pain, falling to the ground, my legs unable to hold my weight when they reformed. I was breathing hard, refusing to cry out with the intensity of the pain of transformation. I felt her claws scrape my insides, looking for a way to be free. Just when I thought I couldn't take it another second, it was over. I stretched in my new body, a black panther.

I turned to go back and almost ran into Stephan. I snorted at him, trying to convey my irritation that he'd watched the whole thing. He turned his head to the side, shaking it in obvious disgust. I growled. He came toward me. Even in panther form he was bigger than me, and I cowered. It was a slight movement on my part, one that I didn't intend, and it made me even angrier. I focused on being still and standing tall as he circled me. My beast was mortified that he was disappointed in us. She wanted control over this body so she could show him that we could do better. It was a struggle to keep her contained.

He came around my side and butted his head against me, marking me with his cheek. My beast instantly relaxed; his show of affection as successful as a hug. Face to face, he gave me a wink and ran off. I sprinted after him. He made it into the trees, and I lost him. I wasn't used to running with anyone, and I had no idea what to do. I attempted to give my beast control slowly, but she broke through my barriers and gained control of our body. I was now an onlooker to her behavior as I had been the first time I'd changed. I could only pray she wouldn't do something unforgivable.

He pounced on us before we had a chance to even start scenting for him, and we growled. We tumbled in the forest, crashing against the brush in a tangled mess of tan and black fur. I shared my beast's joy at being able to play with another. We tricked Stephan into thinking we were going to pin him, and just as he went to brace for our attack, we bolted. We ran full out into the Everglades, not caring that we were on unfamiliar terrain, just loving the chase. We were lithe, graceful, and silent. We began to scent the things around us and take note of the many sounds of the woods.

We jumped over a tree that had grown sideways, deliberately scraping our belly on the top of the trunk before circling back to wait under a palmetto branch for Stephan. We lay there, crouched under the branch in anticipation for hour-long minutes. The tip of our tail twitched in anticipation of our sneak attack. My beast's excitement filled me with such joy, and for the first time since coming back from Atlantis, I was giddy.

He was even stealthier than I, but we were able to hear his soft fur brush against a branch. We crouched farther down, claws digging into the soft soil, tail held straight out behind us. We vibrated with excitement as he walked past, following our scent trail. He was deliberately using only his nose to find us. Had he opened his other senses, he would never have been surprised at our games.

He stopped completely as he reached the tree we had scent marked, belatedly realizing he had entered a trap. We pounced, barreling into his side with enough force to knock over a car. Purring with the impact, we rolled over him and turned for a second attack. He was lying on the ground, shaking his head when we hit again. This time we managed to stay on top of him, biting on the ruff of his neck to declare our dominance over him. He wouldn't have any part of a smaller female dominating him and threw us off easily. We parried about the small area, vying for supremacy, nipping and play fighting with each other until we were panting from exhaustion.

Our stomachs growled, and I nodded my head at Stephan to indicate that I was ready to head back. He shook his head, raising his nose to the air. My beast knew what he wanted us to do, and she was game. Even knowing I forbade it, was appalled by it, she lifted our nose and sniffed. Very faint, there was the scent of small mammals on the air. I screamed my denial yet was ignored. She forced us to our feet and, despite myself, I felt anticipation for the hunt. Sniffing the area for the scent, we pinpointed it and were off.

We maintained a steady tempo until we spotted a den. Stephan nudged our backside in encouragement. I was going to kill him for this. We crept up on the family of grey foxes and pounced before they'd even noticed us. My beast felt remorse, as I did, that they had to die in order for us to eat.

Carrying out the act with as little pain as possible, we killed them quickly, quietly, and respectfully. Taking one by the throat, I felt a sick sense of satisfaction as our teeth sank into the soft flesh. We released him and went for the next, an efficient killing machine. We looked to Stephan for encouragement. I was appalled by what we'd done, but there was another feeling, too. As much as

I wanted to deny it, I was impressed at the delicate simplicity with which the deaths were doled out, at the dignity the poor creatures were afforded.

Stephan sat on his haunches a few feet from us, watching the proceedings with an air of approval. A shiver of joy coursed through us at his support. We nudged a carcass toward him, and he shook his head. We were to eat them all.

We nestled down to start on our meal, glancing up at Stephan to make certain he didn't want to partake. He was a silent witness to our first kill, to my unwilling welcome into the animal kingdom. Our stomach growled—against my will—in anticipation of the fresh meat. The bodies were still warm, blood moistening the meat. I was helpless to stop my beast from gorging on her spoils, yet I could feel everything as she did. The meat was juicy, warm, and delicious to our body. The taste of the blood-coated meat was an exquisite flavor dancing on our palette. The skins were easy enough to rip off, rewarding us with another muzzle full of the tender meat inside. All four foxes were devoured quicker than I could have thought possible.

We were delicate with our meal, not wanting to drop any on the ground and eat more dirt than absolutely necessary. We licked the small droplets off our muzzle, cleaning the rest of our face with our paw, not liking the texture of blood congealing on our fur. I felt full and content for the first time since I''d changed. The experience wasn't nearly as horrible as I'd anticipated. We did what it was that animals do to survive. It was natural, quick, and efficient—not brutal like I'd imagined.

When we finished cleaning our muzzle, we looked back over to Stephan for guidance. We wanted to bury the remnants of the carcasses. We moved our paw in a digging motion, and he snorted. Cocking his head to the side, he shrugged, indicating that we could do whatever we wanted with the remains. We buried them, treating the remains just as respectfully as we did when we killed them. I was grateful that the beast wasn't the monster I'd anticipated, that she had the capacity for compassion.

The trip back to the mansion was subdued and slow. We didn't race each other or try to play. It was a simple walk through the forest that gave me time to think about everything that had happened. If I was being honest with myself, I'd have to admit that I enjoyed the hunt, knowing that I could survive without the aid of another was heady stuff.

Playing, hunting, even killing and eating were all things that I enjoyed with my beast. I wondered if Stephan was right, that she and I really were one and the same. I wasn't sure if I could accept that theory, but I was having trouble completely denying it as well. There was a point during our play where I felt at one with my beast, that the lines of distinct personalities were nonexistent. I felt happy, content, and whole for the first time in my life. I knew that an internal change was on the horizon. I felt an acceptance, an anticipation that I couldn't explain.

As we approached the clearing, I stopped abruptly. I couldn't feel the distinct essence of my beast anymore. There wasn't anyone else sharing my body. I suddenly felt bereft at the loss of my beast even as I realized that she hadn't been a separate entity at all.

With shaking paws, I walked the remaining feet to the clearing where Stephan was waiting. He had already changed and was waiting patiently for me. I wondered if he noticed the difference in me. I wondered if he realized I was walking down the path of acceptance.

"You did better than I'd imagined you would. It's amazing how much you've learned without any guidance. Now, change back so we can get back to the club." He crossed his arms, daring me to hide this change from him. I glared right back. After everything I'd been through tonight, he could have at least let me change in private. I wasn't entirely certain what to do. I didn't feel the same as I had any other time I'd changed. I was more complete in a way I didn't understand.

I sat back on my haunches, closed my eyes, and tried my old technique. Picturing my human form, I braced for the pain. I wasn't prepared for the ease of this transformation. I felt the muscles move, felt that things were occurring to my body that weren't natural, but it didn't hurt. It was uncomfortable, but not painful. It was finished before I had a chance to completely analyze everything. I was left kneeling naked in the grass before a vampire.

I stood, unashamed of my nakedness, pleased at how well I'd done. I inhaled, taking as much of the fresh air into my lungs as possible. I laughed, spinning in a circle with my arms stretched wide in joy. My hair gently moved across my back, the strands causing an involuntary shiver.

"Perhaps our next lesson should be how to return to humanity fully clothed," Stephan choked out. His eyes had darkened. Lust permeated the air, causing me to blush. His hands were clenched in tight fists at his sides, his whole body humming with restraint.

Refusing to feel embarrassed or ashamed, I marched over to my clothes and started getting dressed. I could feel his eyes on me the entire time. A flare of annoyance sparked in me. Had I known I could create clothes, I'd have done so. I didn't particularly want to be seen naked by anyone but Raif.

He was silent. The only indication I had that he was still there was the potent scent of desire permeating the area. It was a thick, heady scent that had my body reacting in response. I desperately tried to ignore it. I knew the reactions were involuntary, knew I didn't love Stephan, but it was just so hard to explain that to my overstimulated hormones.

I finished getting dressed in record time. When I turned back to Stephan, his eyes were dark, stormy pools of magnesium. If I wasn't able to smell the lust pouring off him, I'd have been terrified. As it was, his emotions made me wary of his behavior. My pulse sped slightly in uncertainty. I deliberately held my ground, staring at him in defiance. I refused to feel bad about my ignorance. He could try to intimidate me all he wanted.

"Stephan—" He moved quicker than thought, pinning me to the side of the house before I even realized he'd moved.

"You should not play with things you do not understand. I may be your teacher, I may be ancient, but never forget that I am first and foremost, just a man." His entire body held me captive against the rough siding. My heart thundered in my chest. I had no idea what he was talking about.

"I'm sorry. What did I do?" My voice was soft. He hung his head, touching his forehead to mine, and closed his eyes. He took a few deep breaths, calming his taught body but still holding me captive against the house.

"Forgive me. It's been centuries since I ran with another. I'd forgotten the effects. I was ill-prepared tonight. It won't happen again. We must hurry back. You're not safe with me." His voice was a tight whisper against my cheek.

"What's wrong?" I asked. It suddenly dawned on me—he was hungry. I was alone in the Everglades with a hungry vampire, miles away from anyone. "You're hungry, aren't you?" His eyes flew open. "You can't eat food, can you? That's why you didn't eat with me earlier. Good lord, Stephan. You must be starving." I didn't understand why he hadn't just asked me to open a vein, unless he had to kill to survive. I'd donate a pint or two, but I wasn't willing to die for him. "Do you have to kill when you eat?"

"No." His tone was firm. I wasn't certain if he was answering my question, or if he was denying my unspoken offer. I pulled my hair to one side and tilted my neck toward him. I knew he could see the pulse thudding in my jugular; I could feel the frantic beat. His eyes went straight to the pulse, jaw clenched firmly. His body went even more rigid against mine.

"Then feed."

His mouth latched onto my neck without thought. His hand fisted in my hair, pulling my head back farther. His other hand clenched my lower back, pulling me tightly toward his arousal. He thrust helplessly against me, sucking the life from my body as he did. I gasped, placing my hands on his shoulders to push him away. I'd forgotten the sexual nature of his bite. As my hands gripped his shoulders, I found myself pulling him closer instead of pushing him away, legs weak with my involuntary arousal.

We came together, crying out our satisfaction to the night air. I felt the trickles of blood slide down my neck seconds before he licked the wound closed. He leaned against me, still pinning me to the side of the house. I started to shiver.

"Never again," I whispered. "Promise me this will never happen again." I couldn't even look at him I was so ashamed at myself. No matter how I tried to justify the inadvertent lust, if I ever let him feed from me again, I wasn't sure I'd be able to stop at just the bite. I felt him tense above me.

"Forgive me. I promise." He moved away, walking toward the car with purposeful strides. I sank to the ground, legs unable to hold me up, humiliated with myself and upset that I'd unintentionally hurt him. I'd forgotten what his bite was like. A girl would do just about anything to feel that. I couldn't have him bite me again; he'd wind up killing me, and I'd go, encouraging him until my last breath.

It was a long while before I was able to stand and face him. I got to my feet and walked back to the car. He was leaning against it, body humming with pent up energy. Silently, he opened my door. I offered a small smile as I sat. He was starting the engine before the door even closed.

"Tell me about vampires. Am I going to have to drink blood now that I'm different?"

7

He took so long in answering it surprised me when he finally did.

"No. You don't need to drink blood to survive." He went quiet again. I thought that might be all he would say on the matter, but he sighed as if he'd finally come to a decision. "When Atlantis sank, we were left without the ability to sustain our lifespan. There's something about being Poseidon's offspring that enables us to live longer than humans, but when left without him and without our land, we started aging as normal humans. Before completely abandoning us to his grief, Poseidon wanted to gift us with the ability to maintain our lifespan on the surface. He didn't see how losing most of his offspring, his land, his mate, and then being forced to watch us suffer for a sin we didn't commit was a fitting punishment for his crimes. He thought we'd been punished enough.

"After seeing the devastation meted out to Poseidon and his people by the Fates, the other gods had pity and allowed him to grant this boon, if we so desired. The other gods wanted to make certain that we'd find the act of receiving sustenance difficult, so they placed guidelines, limitations on our gift, convinced that we wouldn't repeat the uprising Atlas achieved.

"Few see vampirism as the true gift it really is. Most would view it as a curse: beings forced to live off another's life force. When we were first given this gift, I agreed that it was a curse, not a blessing.

"We were starving, half mad from being trapped at sea with no place to call home. When we landed in America, we fell upon the first town we came to. The entire village was slaughtered within minutes. Blood drenched our clothing, stained our faces, and filled our bellies for the first time in weeks." He shuddered, the visions of the first kill plainly evident on his face, mortifying him with the memories of the brutality. Pain and remorse coated every word.

"It took years for us to learn that we didn't have to kill to survive. Years of killing humans, just to realize that a mouthful of the sweet nectar would sustain us for the night. By the time we'd discovered this, only fifty of our refugees remained. Twenty more would ask for true death at this discovery, unwilling to live their remaining days with the knowledge that they'd killed hundreds of innocent lives unnecessarily." He went silent again, lost in a pain I hoped to never fully understand, and grieved for those that would only live in his memories. I grieved with him. To have been the cause of so much unnecessary death, and then to be asked to take the lives of close friends...I didn't know how he maintained his sanity.

"You won't have to drink from people because as a Changer, you consume the blood of the creatures you kill. That's one of the reasons why you must learn to be comfortable with hunting in your animal form. The true Atlantean Elementals—the Aeris, Pyros, Nymphs, and Earthen clans must sacrifice one human per year in order to maintain their life, but they do not have to drink daily to survive. They are where your history gets human sacrifices from. Various religions saw what we did and how we maintained our vitality. They attempted to copy our rituals to increase their lifespan, to no avail. Our Elementals are from Atlantis. The power from their element sustains them, but without the Atlantean waters, the elements demand sacrifice.

"I'm an anomaly, as I don't belong to any one clan. There are others like me—the few Necromancers, Dream-Walkers, and Telekinetic Atlanteans—the only ones of our race that don't have a connection to the elements or are able to change, that have to live off the blood of the humans to survive."

"But I Dream-Walked for years before I mated, and I never had to drink blood." I interrupted.

"You were born human. Someone from your lineage must have had offspring with Amphres before he died, and we realized that procreation with humans was possible. It is incredibly rare for a mixed breed to have to rely on the blood of others, but it has been known to happen. That is a lesson for another time.

"I've tried to live off elemental energy, and when that didn't work, I tried living as a Changer. The blood of animals makes me violently ill. The only thing that sustains me is the living blood of another human.

"I'm able to survive with only a pint of blood a week. I prefer the essence of another Atlantean, as it helps maintain my strength and I drink less, but any will do just fine. Taking from the source has always been very erotic for me. It's an uncontrollable, all-consuming, desperate need I try to avoid whenever possible. I'm unsure how others react to their feeding as it is considered rude to discuss." His face flushed, and I was certain mine was crimson.

"You've been the only person in three centuries to cause me to forget myself. Your blood was wonderfully intoxicating when you were human; it was part of the reason I knew you were different. Now that you've become complete, your blood is even more potent. I've only tasted one other who came close to you. With your blood, I may not have to feed for days. I feel energized, my entire body stronger and more vibrant than I've felt in a very long time. It'll be a struggle for me to act human with this power flowing through my veins."

My mouth hung open in astonishment. His candor shocked me. I wasn't used to him being so open with me. More often than not, he was cagey and mysterious about himself.

He glanced over at me and laughed at the expression on my face. His eyes twinkled, dimples deepening on his cheeks; his whole face was transformed with simple joy. Time stood still in that moment. It was in his eyes, the way he held himself. He had enough misery to last a thousand lifetimes, and I was just beginning to understand it all. It made his laugh more precious than others and made me feel special for having provoked it.

"Should I stop, or would you like to hear more?" he asked, coyly glancing at me with laughter still dancing in his eyes. I could barely form the words to answer.

"More, please," I choked out.

"Since you specifically asked about vampires, I'll tell you all you wish to know. Later, I'll teach you about the other clans. You'll need to know everything you can in order to defend yourself against those that would wish you harm." He paused, gathering his thoughts to start explaining my new culture.

"First, there's a difference between natural and created vampires. Natural vampires are the original refugees from Atlantis and our offspring. We aren't undead; we still have souls, and we don't die off during the day." He smirked at me. "Those are always the first questions. We're still the same people we were before Atlantis sank; we just have a different diet. It's still extremely difficult to reproduce, just as it is in Atlantis. The bittersweet irony of being Poseidon's offspring was that while we can practically live forever, reproduction is almost impossible. Poseidon always made absolutely certain that he maintained a certain balance when he gave us a gift. We couldn't benefit from unnatural abilities without giving up something in return.

"Now, a natural vampire is able to walk in the sun; we have reflections, are not affected by garlic, and can enter churches if we so desire. There are few ways to kill a natural vampire, just as there are few ways to kill a true Atlantean. You, *miña mascota*, are a true Atlantean. You have Atlantean blood and were born with a gift. You became what you were truly meant to be when you mated. You became an Atlantean."

"What does that mean?" I interrupted. "If I didn't have my Dream-Walking gift, would I still be single?" Anxiety crept over me; the idea of never knowing Raif hurt to even think about.

"No." Stephan's hand found mine. It was warmer than he usually was. "I believe you would have eventually found each other—it is the soul that matters, not the abilities. However, with you having the blood of Atlantis already in your veins, Poseidon could transport you more easily to Atlantis."

"Oh. Well, what about being a vampire?"

"You must be a descendent of one of the clans to survive the transition into vampirism." I saddened at that. It meant I would most assuredly outlive Katie and Ash. Unless they carried an Atlantean marker and were made into a created vampire.

"We're able to survive almost anything," Stephan continued as if I wasn't already overwhelmed. "Our bodies have superior healing capabilities. You'll find you'll never experience something as trivial as the common cold again. Your body can regenerate any organ or heal any injury as long as your head and heart are intact and connected. The only way to kill a natural vampire, or Atlantean, is to behead them, impale them, or by exsanguination."

"So, the stake through the heart thing is true, but everything else is wrong?" I finally found my voice. He smiled.

"For natural vampires, yes. Things get a bit different with the created vampires." I opened my mouth, but he held his hand up, effectively cutting off my next question. "You really are inquisitive. I'd wondered at your lack of questions earlier. Give me a moment, and I'm certain I will get to it. Natural vampires must feed frequently. How often we feed, and how much, depends on the quality of the blood we take. Like I stated earlier, human blood is the weakest. Atlantean blood is the strongest, depending on the power of the host. Mine, for example is the strongest on the surface. You and your mate would probably be on the same level as Atreyu. He would be the next strongest, following me, but it's impossible for him to visit the surface. Every other natural vamp would follow him, depending on how advanced their power base.

"We can taste the intricacies of individuals. The stronger the host is, the more flavorful the blood. Each person has a unique taste; the powerful Atlanteans pack a kick, regenerating more than just our bodies. The sick and infirm humans taste weak, bitter, and leave a sour note in our mouths. Diabetics and alcoholics are my personal favorites. Their blood is sweet, tangy, and thick with sugar. After drinking, we sometimes know more about our hosts than they are even aware of."

"How so?"

"We can taste the impurities of the blood. Some hosts don't know yet that they're diabetic, or have cancer, for instance. But we recognize the difference as you can recognize the difference between chocolate and steak."

"That's incredible. Think of all the people you could save with early detection if you became a doctor." The possibilities were astounding.

"While we are able to identify the illness, it is poor blood to survive on. And what would the humans think? After a while, word would spread of miracles, and we would have to offer up proof of how we diagnosed something that others could not." Stephan was patient, painting the bigger picture for me. "Humans are to live their lives how they were meant to. We are living ours as best we can without our homeland. To interfere with the natural order of things wouldn't be wise for our survival."

"But—" I began.

"No." He was firm. "It's been tried, and we suffered for it. There are reasons for your myths and stories. There are reasons your kind fear those in power. I will not risk what's left of my people." Silence stretched between us for a moment. All the amazing things they could do for humanity were right there, yet Stephan couldn't—wouldn't—interfere with our lives. Knowing what had happened to Atlantis, I understood. Didn't mean I liked it.

"What about bagged blood?" I asked.

"Bagged blood from blood banks is fine, but the fresher the source, the more potent the blood. As the blood sits, it loses its potency and flavor. I refuse to take directly from the source; it's too erotic. I use stored blood from a high-ranking Atlantean, alternating with freshly donated human blood. I must replenish my stock once a month. You've seen me drink a few times. When I drink in public, I like to have a pitcher of human blood taken from an alcoholic. Their blood is sweet, thick with the toxins of liquor, succeeding in giving me a slightly intoxicated feeling. It's a little joke I like to play while drinking among the humans." He smirked at me and I laughed.

"Created vampires are tricky. They're very different from natural ones in that they were once human like you. Like I stated earlier, only the humans with Atlantean blood running through their veins are able to be made into vampires." I gave him a quizzical look. "Your human traits are dominant to our Atlantean ones. You have Atlantean genes, so you are able to Dream-Walk, but your human genes override the Atlantean ones."

"So I was still fully human until I mated with Raif," I said. Stephan only twitched slightly at the reference to my mate—he was improving.

"Precisely," he said. "A human that holds a trace of Atlantean blood can become a created vampire, joining their Atlantean brethren. They must live off the blood of another, but do not drink as frequently as a natural vampire. They are able to survive, drinking only once a week or so. They're able to walk in the sun for brief periods until they reach five hundred years of age. After that, they're quarantined to the night.

"Garlic is still fine, as are churches." He smiled, dismissing the same litany of stereotypes he did when talking about natural vampires. "They still have their reflections. They cannot reproduce. The healing sleep of the day kills off any abnormality in their body—including a fetus. They don't sleep in coffins, although years ago, it was considered by some to be a wonderful practical joke." He shook his head, and I could tell he was suppressing a smile.

"Created vampires are killed just as easily as humans unless it's close to dawn and they have a sufficient blood source nearby." His voice went soft, reliving some pain I could tell he didn't want to talk about. "They feel things much more intensely than any other creature. When they are pleasured, it's as if every nerve is pleasured at once. When they're in pain, every nerve feels that as well. Their blood doesn't coagulate as a human's. If stabbed or shot, it's possible for a created vampire to bleed to death in minutes." He fell silent. I let him have his moment, knowing that sometimes you had to let the memory wash over you before you could continue. He probably had millions that crept up on him.

"I have not and will not *ever* create a vampire." His voice was firm, answering a question I would never have asked. "Those that are under my protection came to me from a creature that was destroyed. It's beneficial for created vampires to stay in their kiss—their vampire clan. They have the protection and name of the natural vampire, as well as a vast amount of willing donors that have been specifically chosen throughout centuries. The created vampires that attempt to live without a kiss rarely survive long, if at all. They need the structured hierarchy of the group to be held accountable for their actions.

"I'm not entirely certain created vampires retain their souls." His voice was so soft, I could barely hear it over the wind. "I hope they do, but watching them as they age and grow into something heartless leads me to believe otherwise. I would never willingly remove someone's soul. Living as even less than what Hades cursed us to would be beyond cruel." He shook his head.

"I'm getting ahead of myself. Forgive me, I'm not used to explaining our heritage and life to another. The vampires under my protection were taught by their previous masters about their history, abilities, and limitations. I'm trying to remember everything but keep losing myself. Created vampires cannot create another vampire. Only a natural vampire can create a vampire. The madness of our existence reaches created vampires faster than it does us. It's something about the weight of the years combined with their lonely nighttime existence.

"I've never seen or heard of a created vampire finding their soul mate. That, combined with the quick onset of madness, leads me to believe that they may lose the portion of their souls that has the ability to connect with another, in essence, becoming truly undead." He sighed. "It's a mystery I've been trying to solve for centuries." He went quiet and stayed that way until we started seeing the lights of the city. "Do you have questions?"

"Thousands."

"Pertaining strictly to the subject of vampires?" He smiled.

"Okay, let me get this straight. Natural vampires are really just normal Atlanteans that have to drink human blood instead of food, because they're not Changers or part of the Elementals, and created vampires are more like the vampires in the storybooks." He nodded. "So, even though you don't have to, can you eat food?"

"No. Our stomachs rebel at any foreign material other than blood."

"That sucks. I'd be miserable without a pizza or chocolate."

He smiled wistfully at me. "I do occasionally miss the taste of food. Strawberry tarts, the sweet nectar of a durian, chocolate. Perhaps when Atlantis rises and I'm able to return to my homeland, I'll be able to eat food again." He couldn't completely hide the hope in his voice. No matter how angry he was with Raif, I knew then that he was glad the prophecy was being fulfilled.

"Created vampires have to have a trace of the Atlantean bloodline coursing through their veins, right?" He nodded. "How can you tell? I mean, you knew I was different when you met me, but I don't understand *how* you knew."

"That's a difficult question to answer. When you meet the other clans, you'll understand for yourself. The vague answer is that a human feels different from someone with Atlantean blood. As a human, you had an undefined sense of power that radiated off you. Had you remained human, you wouldn't have shown your age until almost near death. Had you led an uneventful life and died naturally, you would've easily lived past one hundred years.

"With humans, you can feel their limitations. It's easier to feel when drinking their blood. They taste weak, bland. The vitality of life is diminished. You can almost smell them dying, feel it as they rub against you. It's difficult to truly explain to someone. It's something you're going to have to understand for yourself. Do I feel different to you than your family back home?"

"Shouldn't they feel like me? If we're related, certainly they have trace amounts of the Atlantean bloodline in them as well, right?" It was the hope I was holding onto since he'd started this conversation, and I was afraid to hear the answer. I couldn't watch Ashlyn die.

"Usually only one member of a family holds the genes of an Atlantean." He explained gently, understanding my pain. "It is highly unlikely that any other living member of your family is like you. Perhaps you've heard stories of an older relative who either went mad or lived in seclusion for many years, dying at an old age, alone? That person would've most likely held the genetic makeup you hold."

I thought about the little I knew of my family. I couldn't think of anyone that fit his description, but that wasn't altogether surprising. "My parents died when Katie and I were young. They weren't close to their families, and I wasn't interested in knowing at that time, I explained absentmindedly.

"Unless discovered and made into a created vampire, the human with our genetic code is usually unable to cope with the abilities they hold. They're confused, bombarded with stimuli that they're unsure of how to filter properly, and tend to exhibit signs of lunacy. Typically, they end their tormented lives within a few years of developing their natural talent. It's one of the reasons we search out the few that have potential and guide or transform them, if they choose, as best as we're able."

"I'm glad I was found." The thought of going crazy from my Dream-Walking or becoming trapped in the Void for eternity wasn't a prospect I found exciting.

"How did your family feel to you, when you returned to them?" he asked, again.

I closed my eyes and thought about Katie over the last three months. I refused to think about Ashlyn; I didn't want to cry. I still held some bitterness toward Katie that enabled me to think of her without breaking down. I tried to remember things I thought of when I smelled her, when I was close to her.

I remembered a sense of her diminished capacity, but it was so much more than that. Her body held a sense of urgency deep in its cells. I heard them scurrying about, racing to complete their tasks as if they, too, felt the limited time a human body possessed. Her heart thundered in her chest, racing to completion before time ran out. She constantly had a faint odor of decay radiating from her. It would never have been scented by another human. I certainly never smelled it until I changed, and even then, it was faint. It struck me that humans may subliminally know of it. Maybe that's why they bathe so frequently and use so many scented products.

Katie had a sense of lightness to her that Stephan did not. I remembered noting that, more than anything else. Stephan and Victoria had an atmosphere of heaviness to them that humans lacked. I started thinking how Stephan felt to me, not emotionally, but metaphysically.

He was still and calm. I wasn't certain yet if it was just his personality, or if it was because he was an ancient Atlantean vampire. His pulse was slower, beating once to every five human beats. He'd always felt more lethargic to me than what I was used to. It wasn't the lethargy humans are used to; it was like he didn't have the same sense of urgency most humans have. He was calm and patient, as if he understood that he really did have all the time in the world to simply exist. He held a heavy weight on his shoulders, as though the years of his eternal existence pressed him down, keeping him rooted in the chaos of humanity. He was the eye of the hurricane.

My eyes flew open in surprise at my discovery. I was staring at the back entrance to the Krypt Keeper. Our time was almost up. We'd have to return to the real world where he was a leader and a businessman.

"I think I understand what you mean." My voice was quiet. I was still thinking over everything I'd learned. I wanted to know more, wanted to spend more time talking about everything, but I was painfully aware that I'd already taken up so much of his time.

"Out with it already," he said. I glanced up at him but didn't respond. My hands were twisting together in my lap, just as my mind was wrestling with what to say. "What's bothering you, *miña mascota*?" I blushed, unable to meet his eyes.

"I'm not sure what I'm supposed to do now. I know you said you'll teach me everything, but you're also a very busy person...vampire...whatever. You're the leader of a kiss and own your own business. Now you have to babysit me. I'm not used to feeling helpless and needy, and I don't particularly like it. I appreciate you putting me up and helping me with everything, but I think I should find my own place, get a job, and continue to live my life. We can make appointments to train, like class. I just don't want to be a burden." I finished with a shrug and looked out the window, still not wanting to meet his eyes.

"Natasha." He spoke so softly and with such compassion I felt like I could have cried. If I'd had tears to shed, one would have certainly been sneaking down my cheek with the intensity of my shame. I silently thanked whoever was listening that I couldn't cry.

I felt his fingers on my chin. They were rough, calloused, yet surprisingly gentle. He turned my face to look at him.

"*Mascota*, you are not, and never will be, a burden to me. I am honored beyond measure that you sought me out for guidance. You have shown more strength, courage, and compassion than any person I've ever met. I know what this is costing you. You've lost everything." He paused, his voice cracking. "I'm a poor substitute for your house, your history, your family. The life you'll never have again. Whatever I'm able to do for you after all you've done for us, know that it is my honor and privilege to do so. You, *miña mascota*, are not a burden." He was unyielding.

I was grateful yet again that I was unable to cry. I'd never looked at my situation in that way before. Never really thought about what I was giving up to be Raif's mate, to have this life. I bit my lower lip to keep it from trembling. That was what I really hated. I looked ridiculous crying without tears. Stephan's eyes darted to my lips, dilating slightly. I only noticed because he still held my chin gently in his hand. We were inches from one another. I could feel a different kind of tension brewing, and I refused to acknowledge it.

"What does that mean? *Miña mascota*? You call me that quite often." It was his turn to blush, just a faint hue, but on his pale skin, it was adorable.

"Little kitten," he whispered. His eyes were swirling with unspoken emotions. His hand moved from my chin to sweep the hair away from my cheek.

"That's cute," I replied as I pulled away, hating what I was feeling, hating even more that I melted at his name for me. "What do we do now?"

If he truly understood the depth of that question, he wouldn't have answered. Hell, I didn't even know if I wanted an answer to it. How was I having feelings for a man when I deeply loved, and was mated to, another?

"I have to check on a few things, and you are welcome to have fun. I ask that you stay in the club, though. Stay in your room or in the bar until you get more training and a better handle on your abilities. You're safe here; outside these walls I cannot guarantee that. If you would like to explore Miami, I ask that you be escorted by either myself or Victoria." I scrunched up my nose in disgust at being babysat. I didn't really care for his options but was trying to understand his concern.

"I think I'll check out your club. I had fun here last time."

With that, we left our first day of training and returned to reality, or a strange version of it at least.

8

Much of the next week was spent the same way. We'd get up in the late afternoon; Stephan would drink his blood; I'd eat more food than any one person should ever eat, and we'd head out to the house in the Everglades. We alternated on the blood situation. If we had a long night and I had to hunt, I'd open a vein in a glass for Stephan, which had become less disgusting as the week went on. If the plan was to play and help me get comfortable in a form that was new to me, he'd drink blood from his thermos. I laughed every time he drank from it, making a mental note to get him new ones that had cartoon characters on them.

I learned quite a bit that week about changing and hunting and was rather proud of my accomplishments. I was no longer separated from my beast. We were comfortably united. Changing was easy, no longer the painful experience of three months ago.

During our more strenuous days, the ones where I hunted and opened a vein, we spent time trying out new things. Every night, we'd change forms; some nights, we'd try as many as four different cats. Those were the rough nights. We'd not only change shape, but he'd make me learn the animal, understand its strengths and weaknesses. We always started the night out as panthers. I'd wondered about that and asked Stephan on our fourth night out. He blushed.

"I like the panther." He stopped, looking mildly uncomfortable. He never made me wait too long, just long enough to get irritated. I think he was trying to rid me of my human tendencies of instant gratification and learn some Atlantean patience. If that was the case, it was going to take all his Atlantean patience to teach it to me. "The panther is the form I'm most comfortable in, other than human. In time, you'll notice that you also have a favored shape. All Changers do. Even if they're able to take on multiple forms, Changers tend to pick one that means something to them, one that matches the core of their character. Changing is our basest of instincts manifesting into animal form."

I smiled, loving that explanation. I thought back to when I first started changing and how my body chose different cats to suit its purpose—the lion to protect Ashlyn, cheetah for running, and the leopard for its playfulness. Each cat had a different purpose at its core.

The panther was a nighttime predator. Its pelt was perfect for concealing itself in the forest. It was also very tuned into family and play. I was slightly surprised at this being Stephan's choice. I'd have thought he would be more like Raif—exotic, endangered, and mysterious, like his black leopard. I never would've imagined Stephan as a family-centered vampire.

After we ran and played for a while as panthers, he would stop and change into something else. Like he had warned me when we started training, changing multiple times a night was exhausting. He would pick another feline for me to copy, one that I already had some knowledge of, and we'd spend the remainder of the night hunting, playing, and getting comfortable in the new body. If I hadn't gotten tired, or if I learned the cat quickly, we'd move onto another. We'd exhausted all the cat creatures I could think of, and I started to wonder when he'd try something else.

We'd been training for exactly a week. It was the night of the full moon, and we both had more energy than normal. I was giddy, laughter bubbling up for no reason. I could feel the currents flowing both through and around my body.

"What are we going to do tonight?" I asked as I danced around the clearing. Stephan smiled. The energy emanating from him was different tonight. "Why do you feel so human?" I asked, unwilling to focus on any one thing.

"It's the moon," he explained. "On nights of the full moon, we become more vibrant. Changers feel the energy more than the other clans. The younger, more untrained, feel the pull so strongly that they *have* to change on nights of the full moon."

I smiled, throwing my arms out, truly enjoying the night. There were currents of energy that I was starting to recognize as we trained—currents that I'd once ignored as unimportant or superstition. Now, they hummed through the earth. The very air tingled against my skin, making me giddy and alert.

"Occasionally, when the moon is closer to the earth—like it will be next month during the red Hunter's Moon—Atlanteans become moon-drunk." He smiled at that. "Lunar eclipses, blue moons, and even the gentle ebb and flow of the natural lunar cycle affects our cellular makeup. While she has no bearing on our ability to change shape, she does hold sway over the energy in our bodies."

"That makes sense. Even humans feel it to an extent." I lifted my head to the sky, closing my eyes to fully enjoy the undercurrents of energy I could feel.

"We become alive with the waxing moon, full of life while she glows full and bright. When she wanes, we become more subdued until the renewal of the new moon, when we start all over again." I hadn't seen him moving closer to me as he spoke. His voice was a whisper against my cheek. "There are subtle changes only another Atlantean would recognize. Having descended from a water deity, our bodies react stronger to the pull of the moon's rays than any other creature. You must learn and adapt to these changes, the desires the moon brings. Can you feel the pull?"

I definitely felt it. Every cell in my body sang with need. It was frustrating and exciting at the same time. I grinned at Stephan, and he winked at me before he ran. Five steps in, he leapt midstride and transformed into a sleek black panther, landing gracefully on all four paws. I laughed. He turned his head, swishing his tail in impatience for me to hurry. He wanted to play.

I wasn't sure if I was quite at that level of changing, but I had to try. Holding onto the image of the form I wanted, I started forward. I took a running leap and changed in midair, body rearranging and molding to fit the image I held, feeling the air currents tickling parts of my body that had never felt a breeze before. I finished just as the ground rose up to meet me.

I didn't land on all four paws gracefully like Stephan. I landed on my front paws, muzzle instinctively tucking under as my back paws flew over my head. Somersaulting in the grass, I finally landed in a heap next to Stephan as his cat made a rough coughing sound, laughing at me. I lay sprawled on my back like a beetle, my tail crimped uncomfortably beneath me.

I laughed with him, my barking cough sounding strange in the clearing. I rolled off my tail and onto my belly to look at him properly. Despite the embarrassing landing, I was thrilled that I'd managed to change into this new creature. Stephan had encouraged me to try, certain that I'd be able to, but with us concentrating exclusively on feline creatures, I hadn't believed him. This body was smaller than I was used to, more compact. The sensory input was different, too. Instead of relying on whiskers and scent, I was relying on sound and scent. Stephan head-butted me, asking if I was okay.

I nodded my wolf's head as I stood up and began to prance around to get used to the smaller creature. I swished my bushy tail and leapt on Stephan. It was a scene for a fairytale, or at least a very bad joke. The panther and the wolf go into a bar… I inwardly laughed at my own poor joke as I tried to knock him over. He was harder to knock down with my smaller weight, but I caught him off guard, and he was chuckling, distracted and amused by my surprising shape.

We tumbled around the clearing for a bit, rolling and nipping at each other. This was the best way to learn the abilities and limitations of an animal—to play and fight with someone I trusted so I'd know how the body would react in life-or-death situations. We both knew we weren't trying to kill one another; it was just play. He was gearing up for another pounce when I bolted.

I ran as fast as my legs would carry me, daring a glance back to see if Stephan was following. He was right on my tail. I let out a little yip of surprise and bolted into the underbrush of the forest. Zigzagging my way around the woods, running in circles and back again, I finally lost him. I ran a bit farther, diving into a thicket of palmettos to wait for him to find me. Chest heaving with exertion, my tongue lolled out the corner of my mouth.

Keeping my ears alert to his approach, I waited. Minutes ticked by and still no Stephan. I knew I wasn't that good. I couldn't have completely lost him. I waited a bit longer, convinced that he was trying to trick me out of hiding and back into the chase. I didn't want to play anymore. I wanted him to find me so we could hunt and go back to the club. I was too full of energy to play as an animal. I itched for something else, something that was more complex than the simple needs of my animal nature. I wanted to play as a person, with another person. I wanted Raif and the things only he could do to me. Since I couldn't have that, I wanted to dance and feel someone else's sweat on me.

My panting subsided as I thought about what the rest of the night would bring and worried about Stephan's lack of appearance. He'd never made me wait this long before. Tentatively, I stepped out of my hiding spot. Lifting my nose, I scented the air. Nothing. Following my trail backwards, I tried to find exactly where I'd lost him. Maybe this was a new lesson? I needed to learn my wolfish ability to track and hunt; maybe this was Stephan's way of teaching me. If it was, it royally sucked, and we were going to have words later.

I picked up his scent when I reached the area where I'd run in circles. He wasn't alone. Another female had discovered us, and from the scent path, Stephan had taken her back to the house. My hackles raised in anger. How dare he! This was our territory. I hunted here; we played. I felt safe and welcome here in a way I never had anywhere else. How dare he bring another woman into my den!

I stormed through the woods, temper rising with each step. I was furious. The house was close, only about a mile away, when I started feeling uneasy. The hairs on my scruff and between my shoulder blades started to prickle. I stopped to figure out why.

Sitting down, I scented the air and listened to the birds. Their chattering was muted, warning others of the brewing tension. I didn't smell anything out of the ordinary, though. My ears swiveled to listen for the cause of the disturbance, still unable to place it.

Thinking about Stephan and the woman, I started on again, ignoring the lingering unease of my surroundings. I couldn't believe he'd bring someone back there. Our training grounds, my home, he... I stopped so suddenly I almost fell over myself.

I didn't have a home.

This was Stephan's house, his property, to do with as he pleased. I was just his guest and his student. He was a grown man. If he wanted to bring someone else here, I had no right to complain. Although, I didn't quite understand why he'd bring a woman here instead of the bar. With the full moon upon us, though, I didn't question the erratic behavior.

Depressed now, I didn't know what to do. I didn't want to interrupt them, but I didn't want to hide out in the forest alone, either. I wished I had a place of my own, a place that I could go to where I was safe, protected, and cared for. I was suddenly, overwhelmingly homesick. I missed Katie and her pain-in-the-butt habits. Her inability to understand and deal with anything out of her own little skewed view of the world would be a balm on my weary soul.

I missed Ashlyn. That kid was the sun itself. I'd give up everything to just be able to go back and read horrible bedtime stories to her, both of us oblivious to the reality between the pages.

Placing my head on my front paws, I lay in the woods. For the first time since leaving my family, I mourned them. I was alone. Completely lost in a world that was so different from what I knew, I was utterly alone and homeless. The only person that could ease my heartache was trapped on an island hidden in the depths of the ocean. Tearlessly, I wept, hating everyone and everything that had happened since that fateful day.

It was strange to cry as a wolf, without tears. Mostly, I just huffed and snorted, nose running and chest heaving. I cried at the loss of my tears, just another thing that marked me as different— freakish. I cried at the stupidity of crying. I cried until I was all cried out and emotionally drained.

I had to go back. It was time. Surprisingly, I felt better after my bout of weeping, just very tired. I no longer wanted to go back to the club and dance. I wanted a cheeseburger and my bed. Surely the woman would be gone by now, and Stephan and I could go back to the bar where I at least had a small sense of self.

My tail hung low to the ground as I walked back to his house. I kept reminding myself it was his, not mine, and I had no reason to be upset. It was the longest mile I'd walked in a long time. During that time, I made a vow with myself to find a place I could call mine. I didn't need much, a small cottage and room to run. Maybe John would help me find something. He always seemed eager and excited to help. I'd ask him tomorrow if he would. Feeling better from the cry and knowing I had a tentative plan set in motion, I was more relaxed as I walked into the clearing.

I emerged from the woods, head high and tail wagging slightly with renewed purpose. Stephan and the woman sat across from each other on the small outdoor patio. From my spot at the edge of the woods, I could tell that the woman was speaking, and Stephan was listening intently. My steps faltered just a bit. They didn't notice. I walked around the pond, reassuring myself and trying to maintain my calm acceptance. This woman obviously knew Stephan, was on friendly terms with him, and wasn't any of my business.

I knew the minute Stephan noticed me. He stiffened slightly, then relaxed almost immediately. The woman continued to prattle on, seemingly oblivious to my entrance. When I was close to the patio, Stephan interrupted her, speaking clearly and loud enough that I could understand.

"Sonja, please forgive me. It appears Natasha has decided to join us after all. I wasn't expecting you tonight and have not had a chance to discuss this with her. If you'll excuse me for a moment." He didn't bother waiting for a response. He stood and walked toward me. Sonja smiled at him, turning to get a quick glimpse of me as he walked over. Her eyes widened in surprise.

I watched them with a wary disposition. Sensing my unease, Stephan walked slowly toward me, palms open in a nonthreatening manner. I didn't like the tension in the air and wanted to bolt. It took everything I had in me to wait for him to approach. The wolf's instincts were stronger and harder to control than my feline ones. Either that, or I still needed more time adjusting to my dual nature.

"Natasha, I meant to talk to you about this before Sonja came, but apparently things progressed faster than either of us had anticipated. I hope you can forgive me the awkwardness of this introduction. Please come into the house with me for a moment so I can try to explain. You're still safe. Sonja means you no harm and she's alone." He held his hand out, waiting for me to take it. His voice was soft, pitched low so only I would hear him.

I snorted. He was an idiot if he thought I was going to change in front of this woman. Head-butting his hand, I felt him stroke my pelt down to my tail as I walked past him to the house. The rear door opened into a mudroom of sorts, where there were still large washbasins complete with hand cranks and washboards to clean with. It was a long, thin room, spanning the length of the house and only about six feet wide. I hadn't been in the house since our first night here, and this room was a surprise.

I was sniffing around one of the basins as Stephan walked in, shutting the door behind him. He waited for me to finish my self-guided scent tour, knowing I would change back into a human when I was ready and not a moment sooner.

I thought about what I'd been learning, thought about the nicely dressed woman outside, and tried my best to have clothing on when I changed back. This had proven to be somewhat of a challenge for me in recent days. I could understand fur, skin, and the various intricacies of different animal forms, but for the life of me, I kept getting stuck on the clothing concept.

The transformation was quick. One moment I was a wolf, the next I was me. I was still crouched on the ground with my eyes closed, concentrating on the finer details of a long dress. Stephan, as usual, was waiting patiently for me to finish and acknowledge him. I opened my eyes and stood, hoping I was finally successful with the whole clothing thing.

"Very good." He smiled at me, satisfied that I'd finally managed to get myself covered.

I stood barefoot in a knee-length red dress. It wasn't exactly what I'd been trying for, but at least this time all my bits were covered. It was a vast improvement over the past few nights. I looked back up at Stephan, refusing to be distracted by a stupid dress.

"Who is she?"

"Forgive me, Natasha." He bowed his head, baring the side of his neck to me. Great, he must be really upset to revert to such formality. He never used my full name, and certainly never bowed to me. I started to worry. "I wasn't expecting Sonja for another week, at least. I was planning on spending that time to talk to you about this. I wanted to run, get the moon's pull out of our systems, but she surprised me. Sonja is a Nymph, and my attorney. It seems as if she was able to process my request faster than anticipated and was eager to meet you with the good news. It was not my intention to surprise you in this manner."

"Why's she here?" He was doing his formal speak thing again, something he only did when he was uncomfortable. "Why does seeing her have you so upset?"

"I am only concerned for you and your reaction. I do not wish to see you troubled." He sighed. "You told me once that you felt like a burden, that I was a busy, important vampire who didn't need to babysit you, or some such nonsense." I blushed at the reminder. "I told you this was my home and that I owned and ran the Krypt Keeper. I fear I may have misled you by omitting a few details. Over the many years of my long existence, I've accumulated a vast empire. This is my home; however, it's not the only one I have. Truth be told, I own property in every nation in the world. The Krypt Keeper's where I run things, simply because it's the only safe home in Florida, and I prefer to be close to the Atlantic Ocean. It makes me feel closer to Atlantis. I'm the leader of a kiss, but it's more than that. I'm the leader of all of the Atlanteans that remain on the surface." His hands ran up and down my arms, distracting me slightly from what he was saying.

I'd learned over the past few days that touch was important to Stephan. He didn't touch many people, but when he did, it was to comfort either himself or them. I wasn't entirely certain who he was trying to reassure here. He knew I wanted to keep to myself, that my interactions with other Atlanteans hadn't been positive and I didn't care to meet more.

For him to spell out where he was in the power structure was intense. If it were anyone else, I'd have thought he was trying to impress me. I knew he was powerful, and I knew on a subliminal level that he was formidable, but being the leader of an entire race on earth was more than powerful.

"I didn't want to overwhelm you with so much all at once. I've lived for over eleven thousand years. I've had time to procure wealth, to build my empire. I've had time to become the leader my people needed. I've—"

"Why are you telling me all of this?" I whispered, unable to speak any louder.

"I know how you are," he whispered back. "You are a strong, independent woman who doesn't want to rely on others. You've shown me your steel core time and again. I know, more than you realize, what you're going through, what you're giving up for our people." His voice was thick with pain, allowing me a glimpse of what he hid from the rest of the world. The whole time he talked, he caressed my arms, subconsciously pulling me closer to him until I could feel the curves of my body lining up with the hard lines of his. He cleared his throat. "I want you to know that all of that, my position, power, wealth—it means nothing to me. You are returning my homeland to me, to all Atlanteans. I want to show you my gratitude by giving you back something you've lost."

I looked up into his magnesium eyes. Not for the first time, it was difficult to ignore the underlying tension between us. Looking into his eyes, I knew that the more time I spent with him, the stronger this pull would be, and I hated myself for feeling this way.

He was vulnerable, open to me in whatever way I wanted. I could read the invitation etched in every part of his face. His eyes swam with an emotion I knew he'd never express. And I wanted it. Gods be damned, for the first time since finding Raif, I wished I was free to feel what I felt for Stephan. But how could I feel anything for someone who wasn't my mate? How could this craving surpass the love I felt for Raif? I closed my eyes to block out the temptation staring back at me. I had to focus on what Stephan was saying.

"I don't understand."

"I want to give you a place to call your own—a home."

"You're giving me a house?" I squeaked out, eyes fluttering open in shock. He nodded. "I can't accept that, Stephan. It's too much. People don't just give houses away!" First, he was the most powerful being on the planet, then he was the leader of the most powerful creatures on the planet, next, one of the wealthiest people in the world, and now he wanted to give me a house.

"People don't give up their very existence to help a band of mythical ancient warriors either," he replied, very softly. "Tasha, you forget your worth. You, *miña mascota*, are truly a rare gem. I don't understand how Raifuku was able to let you go so easily."

I winced at his callous words. It wasn't an easy parting. I let it go, though, partly because of my inexcusable, fluctuating emotions, and partly because I just didn't want to argue.

"Please, allow me to do this one small thing for you. Let me give you a place to call home." His eyes pleaded with me. I didn't know what to say. I was completely numb from shock. Somehow, I managed a small nod.

He smiled, kissing my forehead before leading me out to the table where Sonja still sat, waiting patiently for us to return. She smiled at us, standing as we approached. She was beautiful. I hadn't really noticed as a wolf, the colors skewed through my animal eyes. She was well over six feet tall, thin, and had tight, firm breasts accented by the deep blue halter dress she wore. Her long, strawberry blond hair was pulled back into a tight ponytail. Her wide, sapphire blue eyes shone with an internal humor. She held a long, delicate hand out to me. Numbly, I shook it.

"It truly is a pleasure to finally meet you. The whole community has been buzzing about your arrival. We've all been wondering about the one who finally fulfilled the prophecy." She sat as Stephan led me to another chair and held it for me. The fog was slowly lifting from my mind, leaving behind the knowledge that I was finally meeting another Atlantean—and she *wasn't* trying to kill me.

"I apologize for arriving unannounced. I was just so thrilled to be able to expedite this for you." She beamed at me, expecting admiration, I guessed. "Also, I just really wanted to meet you." She blushed a deep crimson that finally succeeded in making me smile.

"Let's get this taken care of. Natasha and I still need to hunt tonight." Stephan's rough tone surprised me a bit. Sonja took it in stride.

She pulled up a thick black briefcase stuffed with paperwork. We spent the next hour signing, initialing, and legalizing the transfer of one of Stephan's homes to me. I couldn't wait to see it. I felt a tad guilty, but desperately tried to ignore it. I knew he was trying to be nice, and I didn't want to be rude. I was also thrilled that I now had a place where I could go to run, to be myself without the strange looks. I smiled as the last page was signed.

"All right then, everything's settled. I'll file these tomorrow. You should have your new title in a few weeks. Stephan, I trust you'll give her the keys later?" He nodded, and she continued. "Do you know when you're going to have your coming out party?" She asked me as she gathered her paperwork.

"My what?" I asked. Stephan had the grace to blush.

"Your coming out party. It's a celebration into a new vampiric life. All the created vamps have one before they turn. If they have it after, well, things tend to get messy. I know you're not a vampire, but you must have a party. People are dying to meet you." She laughed at a joke I didn't understand. I smiled, shrugging as I looked at Stephan.

"I hadn't thought about it," he said, still embarrassed at his obvious social blunder. Sonja gasped, hand fluttering to her throat as her mouth gaped open in astonishment. I ducked my head to avoid laughing at her.

"Stephan! You can't keep her hidden all to yourself. She needs to meet the rest of us, see for herself that we're not all like that dreadful Stuart." She glanced at me, her expression of pity quickly replaced by one of excitement. "I know. Have it here during the Hunter's Moon next month. We can all get moon-drunk and celebrate properly. It'll be wonderful!" She beamed at the thought. I thought it sounded fun but was nervous at the idea of being around so many people.

"That sounds like a wonderful idea. I'll get John on it immediately. You know how he likes to plan a party." Stephan smiled at Sonja. With that decided, I said farewell to my first Nymph. Life certainly wasn't dull anymore.

9

We drove off shortly after Sonja left, as I wasn't in the mood for hunting. Stephan was his usual gracious self and stopped by a fast-food place so I could load up on greasy protein and carbs. He silently nursed his thermos of blood as I inhaled my third double cheese. It was awful and oh-so-yummy at the same time. The Miami lights came into view, and I had to disrupt the peaceful silence.

"So, where's my house?" I asked around a mouthful of burger. Stephan coughed, a spray of blood hitting the dash.

"What do you mean? It's the house we just left. I thought you knew." He looked astonished as he mopped up the droplets of blood with one of my napkins. It was my turn to choke.

"What? That place is huge! I thought you were giving me an apartment in the city or something. I can't take that house. Besides, it holds memories for you." He had to be joking.

"It's already done. John will go out with you tomorrow and help you figure out how you're going to fix it up. It's been empty for three hundred years; it's about time someone lived in it. It'll need electrical, plumbing, and I don't know what else. John has updated property for me before. He'll be happy to help you."

We drove the rest of the way to the club in silence. Just when I thought I was getting used to my new life, a curveball was thrown at me. Usually by Stephan.

I went straight to my room as soon as we arrived at the club. I was exhausted and needed some time to myself to decompress after such a strange day. I flung myself on the bed and closed my eyes. I was out in seconds.

"Miss Natasha, we have to get going. I've arranged for people to meet us out at the house in two hours for your orders. They're going to be irritated if they have to wait for you. We have to get going." He shook my shoulder again, and I blinked up at him. It looked like John but seemed different somehow. John wasn't usually so blunt with me. I must have really overslept.

"What time is it?" I asked, voice thick and groggy with sleep.

"Seven." Great. I'd had about three hours of sleep. It felt like five minutes. "Breakfast is waiting for you downstairs. You need to hurry, or you won't have time to look at the house before the crew gets there." He left me to bathe and dress in private.

I was putting my shoes on when he returned. He walked in, not bothering to knock. I was surprised at his rude behavior; it wasn't something I was used to from John. Maybe he wasn't a morning person.

"Are you ready yet? I had the cook put breakfast in a bag so you can eat it on the way. Let's go." He left without waiting for an answer, completely missing the growl I gave him.

I didn't think it was possible, but he drove faster than Stephan. Usually, I liked the speed, the wind blowing my hair all around and the trees whipping past us, but today, I was terrified. I couldn't eat as he moved through the city at speeds unsafe even for closed circuit racing. He didn't slow for lights, swerved around pedestrians, and took turns on two wheels. My knuckles were white from the tension. When we returned to the club, I was going to have to figure out how to explain to Stephan why his car door handle had fingerprint dents in it.

I leapt out of the car as it skidded to a stop in front of the house, collapsing on the grass, grateful to be still at last. John laughed and tossed a flashlight toward me. Without even a glance back at me, he went up the stairs and into the house. I was never going anywhere with him again. I sat on the grass for another minute before my legs stopped shaking enough to hold my weight.

Grabbing the flashlight, I headed up the steps to the massive entryway.

It was even more spectacular in the light of day. John had left the double doors cracked open, and I pushed them as far open as they would go. I pulled open the heavy curtains, letting in more sunlight, setting the dust motes sparkling. It was beautiful. Cobwebs glittered in the sun's rays, and bats screeched as they flew toward a darker habitat. It was the perfect house from an old horror film. I loved it.

Smiling for the first time that day, I went over to a door on the left, pushing it as far as it would go. With the flashlight's dim glow, I saw more curtained windows. I sneezed as I opened them. This room was huge and lined floor to ceiling with books. There was space only for a fireplace and a bay window, with books covering every other available surface of wall. It was heavenly. My steps echoed on the hardwood floors as I walked through the dusty library. There were three candlestick chandeliers hanging from the ceiling, each with dried wax dripping from the holders. I was afraid to touch anything for fear I'd destroy some valuable tome.

I wandered through the rest of the house, as though in a dream. I found the kitchen that housed an old wood stove, a tub for water, and a large pantry. In the dining room, I discovered an old-fashioned high chair that made me shiver. Something horrible had happened here that Stephan didn't want to discuss. Dinner plates still graced the table.

The first floor also had a ballroom, the mudroom that I'd changed in yesterday, and a door that I assumed led to the basement. Everything was covered in a thick layer of dust.

Once I was satisfied with the first floor, I headed up the ancient staircase. The wood creaked under my feet, threatening to collapse with the added weight of my body. The staircase ended in a hall with a balcony that overlooked the downstairs foyer.

Each door opened into a large bedroom. I noted a bedroom with a crib, but didn't go in. I opened all the curtains in the other bedrooms and checked out the stability of the two balconies I'd found off two of them. Ideas were hitting me in every room as to what I wanted to do with the renovations. I had no idea where John had scampered off to, but after dealing with him that morning, I was glad he'd left me alone.

I started hearing voices outside, so I headed back down the staircase. John was there, rounding everyone up. He'd gathered an architect, an electrician, a plumber, and a carpenter. John himself held a clipboard and pen poised for instruction. It was the first useful thing I'd seen him do all day.

"Hi. I'm Natasha." I smiled and waved at the men. They all gaped back. I turned to see what had their attention, and all I saw was the foyer. It was amazing, so I didn't blame them for gaping. "Okay, then. I guess we should get started. I'll tell you what I'd like done, and you tell me if you can do it. First, the entire house needs electrical and plumbing. It will also need a septic system. Now, in here," I walked into the foyer, "I'd like to convert this closet into a small half bath."

No one was paying attention to what I was saying. John was writing furiously, but the other guys were scrambling over themselves to be close to me. I thought one of them was even starting to drool. I scrunched up my nose and walked over to John. He didn't even glance up as I came over.

"What's going on?" I asked in a stage whisper.

"It's your aura." He didn't so much whisper as sigh, acting as if it was something I should already know. When I didn't say anything more, he looked up to see my confused expression. "Stephan didn't tell you?" He sighed again at my headshake. "Everyone has an aura. Now that you're...different, your aura's different too. It packs more of a punch."

"Why aren't you affected by it?" He sighed deeply; a look of irritation plastered on his face.

"I'm a servant." He said the word as if he'd eaten something rotten. "My family grew up with your people. We're bred to basically assist you with the things you can't do. My ancestors all helped Stephan, and now it's my job. We're immune to your aura. I've been around the clans since I was a baby and can ignore the pull you have. Stephan should've explained all this to you before allowing you out in public."

"Well, it seems as if we haven't gotten to that particular lesson yet," I explained, my tone getting bitchier by the minute. "He's been kind of busy teaching me to not eat people. How do I turn it off?"

His lip curled in disgust. It was an expression I'd never seen John make, especially directed toward me. Gone was the sweet kid I'd met the first night I was here. If this was how he normally behaved, I didn't want him anywhere near me. I didn't trust myself around him. I held too much anger to deal with an attitudinal jackass.

"How should I know? I'm not one of you. You should figure it out, though, if you want anything accomplished today besides making drones." He lifted his clipboard back up, effectively dismissing me.

I tried really hard to hold back my growl. Closing my eyes, I thought about my aura. I thought about the things I'd heard about auras in passing. From what I knew, auras were colorful shields that covered the body. I imagined mine as a light of sorts that pulled men to me like a moth to a flame. I pictured the flame dimming. As the sweat started breaking out on my skin, I pictured a cover on the flame, hiding it from everyone. My eyes flew open in surprise when I felt a noted difference in my body. I felt hidden, like I was only a partial person. It was awful.

I looked at the men around me and sighed in relief. It seemed to be working. They were no longer looking at me as if I was a raincloud and they were parched. In fact, they now held expressions of mild annoyance.

I was going to have to make this quick. Sweat was already trickling down my back. Suppressing my aura was actually harder than my initial experiences with changing. I had to remember to talk to Stephan about this. I sighed as I thought briefly about everything Stephan still had to teach me. The list seemed endless.

"As I was saying, I'd like that closet converted into a small half bathroom. Through here," I went into the dining room, walking stiffer than normal, "I'd like this room shortened a bit, to make the kitchen larger. I'd like recessed lighting and a place to hang an upgraded chandelier." I directed the workers throughout the entire house, dictating what I wanted done and discussing possible variations that would work better. I was drenched in sweat when we finished and visibly trembling. I needed them gone. "When do you think we can start?"

"We can start with the gutting tomorrow. It should take about six to twelve weeks to complete the renovations." The architect seemed to be the one in charge, and I watched as the others nodded in agreement. I was both excited and disappointed at the same time. It wouldn't be finished before the party, and I wasn't looking forward to holding back my aura for another twelve weeks. I was about to thank them when John piped up.

"As was explained during our phone call, with what Mr. Stephan is paying you for these renovations, you will complete them in two weeks. Good day, gentlemen." My jaw dropped. He turned and walked out of the room, effectively cutting off the complaints that were starting to rise out of the workers.

They grumbled as they left, each casting a stressful look back at the house as they drove off. I barely held onto my anger and my aura until the last of the cars rounded the bend.

"John! You pompous, arrogant ass. How dare you treat people like that. I thought you were nice when I first met you, but now?" I whirled on him, screaming in his face. He held up his hand.

"You can't be serious. You don't actually think I'm that sniveling waste of space, do you? Stupid, ignorant woman! Use your nose. My brother was too busy today serving Victoria to be bothered with you. I'm James." He shook his head, his disdain for me and for being here plainly evident on his face. Muttering about useless females, worthless Atlanteans, and something about my lineage, he turned his back on me. As he walked off, he made one last comment under his breath. "Stupid, useless, Atlantean bitch."

I lost it. After no sleep, no breakfast, and an entire morning of holding back a part of myself, my control was slim as it was. Add to it the constant rude comments and disrespect, and I completely lost it. Without thought, I changed into a panther in the blink of an eye, seeing red as I let out a deafening roar. He turned just in time to see me with fangs bared and claws extended as I pounced.

Landing firmly on his chest, my front paws pinned his upper arms while my back paws straddled his legs. He squirmed underneath me until he felt the tips of my claws graze his skin. I growled, spittle dripping from my jaw. As I bared my fangs inches from his face, he finally understood how stupid it was to piss off a newly transformed Atlantean Changer. Fear clogged the air as the sharp tang of urine wafted from his groin. My growl deepened with the growls of my stomach.

I was starving, and he smelled like dinner. I wanted to rip him apart, taste his blood, and feel the tender flesh as it split in my mouth. I had to know if he tasted as good as he smelled. He sure wasn't worth anything else to me. I licked his face, catching his salty tears in the process.

"Natasha, no! James, what the hell did you do to her?" As John's familiar voice came closer, I growled again. I wouldn't be distracted from my meal. Not when it smelled this good and I was so unbearably hungry. I could barely think past the stench of fear. A small trickle of drool slipped from my jaw as I forced myself to focus on John and not the hunger or the delicious, warm body beneath me.

"Gods be damned, Natasha, stop! You don't want to do this. You're not a man killer. You don't want to do this." John pleading voice held a tiny thread of fear as he started opening something. Hearing a faint click followed by a slight scraping noise, I looked over. It was a sound I was all too familiar with. Stephan's thermos was being opened.

"I have something for you, but you have to come here to get it." Firm resolve covered the slight tremor in John's voice.

He had a platter on the ground, next to a cooler. Seeing that he had my attention, John bent down and opened the cooler. A smell was released that was even better than the stench of urine-soaked fear. Fresh, unsoiled, bloody meat. I stopped growling. As John placed the slab of beef on the platter, I stepped off his brother.

John held up the thermos again. My stomach clenched in anticipation. Warily, I looked at him, this boy who looked exactly like the one I'd wanted to eat, and I waited to see what he was going to do with the thermos. He poured its contents onto the slab of raw beef like barbeque sauce. I leapt over to the blood-soaked treat, purring in contentment as I lapped up every drop of the delicious, still-warm blood. I glanced up at John in between bites, hoping he realized how thankful I was to him.

"What the hell man? That bitch almost ate me," James screeched at his brother, stupidly drawing my attention back to him once more. I growled at him, hackles rising in warning, pausing as I licked the blood from my whiskers. John placed a restraining hand on my head, gently scratching behind my ear and distracting me once again from his idiot brother.

"James, I think you'd better go before she really does eat you. I'm out of treats and she doesn't seem to like you very much." John deliberately kept his voice low, calm, and soothing so I wouldn't become more agitated. He never let up on the scratching.

James finally took his brother's advice, sending one more hate-filled glance my way as he walked by us. I bared my teeth and pretended to jump at him. He ran the rest of the way to his car.

If I hadn't been enjoying the attention from John so much, I'd have run after James and finished the job. He should've known better than to run from a predator, especially when he reeked of fear. It was a temptation I wouldn't have been able to resist five minutes ago.

I closed my eyes as I heard James's car start and peel out of the driveway. Leaning into John as he rubbed my shoulders, I purred in contentment. My shoulders arched and my purr deepened. This was heaven. He laughed as my tail wrapped protectively around his body.

"Like that, huh? Would you mind joining the human population again so we can talk?" I sent him a sad-eyed look. He laughed again. "You make a beautiful panther, and this is certainly not something I do every day, but I would very much like to have a conversation with you that's not one-sided."

I sighed, licking his cheek just before trotting into the library to change back. Clothing was still somewhat of an issue. I made absolutely certain my clothes were in place before heading back into the foyer.

"I'm sorry about trying to eat your brother," I started as I walked out of the room. "I've never attacked a person before. I've never wanted to. I'm still not entirely certain what came over me." I blushed, feeling guilty for causing John stress. I didn't really care that I'd scared his brother. I only cared that I'd upset John. I liked him. He was a good guy, one that I was starting to respect.

"I'm sure he deserved it. I know Stephan's had to put him in his place a few times. I came out here as soon as I found out he was with you. I'm sorry for the way he treated you. He doesn't really like anyone except Victoria. She can't feed off him every week though, so she rotates. Last night was supposed to be one of the other servants, but he's sick, and she doesn't like the taste of medicated or ill blood. Not that I blame her. I'm rambling, sorry." He blushed and grinned. I grinned back.

"All of this is still so new and fascinating to me. You can ramble all you want. I never realized how much everything affected the taste of blood." I laughed. "Thank you for stopping me. I wanted to kill him. I was getting ready when you arrived. Whose blood did you bring?" I shuddered to think what would have happened if he'd arrived a minute later.

"It would have been his own fault if you had eaten him. I'm glad you didn't, though. I'll have a talk with Stephan about him again, make sure he doesn't ever allow James around you. When I realized James was with you, I told Stephan."

"He couldn't come, but opened a vein and filled the thermos, knowing it was a sound you'd recognize. We both hoped you wouldn't need the contents. He had to finish his meeting and feed before leaving. The blood loss is never easy for him, but he'll never admit it," John said. "You should learn my scent so you can tell us apart. James and I are perfect identical twins. We even have the same birthmark. I don't know what Stephan's going to do with him, but I know you can't mistakenly go out with him again. You aren't safe around him."

"I feel stupid for asking this, but how? I've only scented someone as a cat, never as a person. I know your smell, I think. James smelled like you, but off... I thought it was just me being tired." I focused on the conversation at hand, at the new experience, being able to learn something else about my life now—anything except that I'd drank of Stephan's essence and the warring emotions that brought out in me.

He smiled. "It's great that you're familiar with my scent, but getting to my base scent, the heart of who I am, is different. I'm sure you've done it before without realizing it." John grinned. "I'll walk you through it. It's basically the same concept as scenting when you're an animal, but you don't sniff my crotch." I blanched at that idea, and he laughed.

"I don't even do that when I'm a cat!" He didn't hear me over his laughter.

"I feel the same way, so we do this a little differently than animals. You have to get very close to me, bring your nose so that it's touching my neck, inhaling at the vein and my hairline. The sweat glands are potent there, so you can get a good whiff of my personal scent, not my cologne. I also left without bathing, so that should help." He laughed again at my disgusted expression.

Walking up close to him, I could tell he was as nervous as I was. I tried to think of it clinically, ignoring the fact that I was pressing my body tightly against his. Placing one hand on his shoulder and the other behind his head, I pulled him to me. He wasn't that much taller than me; my face fit perfectly in the crook of his neck. Feeling the pulse thundering beneath my lips, I inhaled. I breathed in his scent, gathered it inside me so I would remember it always.

His breath stuttered, and he grabbed onto me for support, not exactly upset about being scented. I tried to ignore his body's response against my thigh as he clutched me tighter to him, suppressing a groan and softly apologizing for his reaction. He started to break out in a light sweat.

I leaned in again, inhaling more of him, memorizing the exact hint of his flavor. It was coated with nerves, stress, and desire, but I could still taste the base scent underneath. He smelled sweet and dusty, like sagebrush in the fall. My lips curled against his skin in a smile. I'd gotten it.

There was the creak of a floorboard, and both John and I looked up. Stephan was standing in the doorway.

10

I leapt away from John as if I'd been electrocuted. We weren't doing anything inappropriate, but I felt as if I'd just been caught having sex in church. I wanted to grovel at Stephan's feet, beg for forgiveness. I stayed put. I knew I didn't have anything to beg for.

Anger radiated off Stephan in waves. His eyes swirled, hands held immobile in tight fists by his side. Storm clouds rumbled outside as a breeze whipped across the threshold. He shook with the effort it took to simply stand still. Never once did he take his enraged eyes off me.

John leaned against the wall, trying to steady his shaking legs so he could walk out. He looked pale, terrified of what Stephan might do to him. His terror spiked my protective instinct and I bristled.

"I was just scenting him." My voice was quiet but strong.

"I know. John, you have to leave. It seems as if I'm not myself today. You may help Marcy for the remainder of the week, if you would like." John nodded, keeping his eyes downcast even though Stephan had yet to look in his direction. Slowly, with deliberate steps, he walked past Stephan and out the door. Only after he drove off did Stephan start to relax.

"Tasha, forgive me. I don't know what's come over me. It seems as if I'm not myself when it comes to you. Did you get things settled today?" The clouds started to clear. His hands unclenched, and his eyes slowly returned to their normal molten silver.

"Yes, but I almost ate James." He looked at me with a raised eyebrow. I explained what happened. By the time I came to the end, where I was scenting John, our anger had returned. My anger

85

was directed toward James for triggering my beast, with myself for how much I had to learn, and a little with Stephan for the gaps that still remained in my knowledge. I wasn't sure what he was so angry about. I needed to run or have violent sex to reaffirm all was well in my world. My irritation increased with my lack of options.

"Do you want to go running with me?"

He nodded. Following me into the backyard, he waited for me to change, and we were off. I ran as fast as my leopard's body could, Stephan close to my heels, letting me set the pace. The tension of the day released as my muscles heated with exertion. We ran for miles, entering territory I loved, and continued to run. I ran until I was on fire, thoughts and emotions being too complex to handle. Slowly, I came to a stop. I was panting, my chest heaving from the run. Stephan glanced over at me, tongue hanging out of his mouth in exhaustion. He head-butted me, rubbing his face against mine in affection, scent marking me as he did so.

Together, we walked leisurely to Lake Okeechobee to get a drink of water. It was on the northern edge of the property line and one of my favorite spots. I was hungry as well, but too tired to do anything about it. I'd hunt after we had a chance to cool off and relax. In the meantime, I simply enjoyed the exhaustion and the freedom I had in this body. I savored this feeling, knowing I could escape from reality and become something different, something that didn't worry about the infinitesimal things humans worried about. The only things I cared about in animal form were in regard to my survival.

It didn't take long for us to reach the water's edge and drink. I could feel the heat radiating off my pelt, and the cool water was a balm to my empty stomach. Contented at last, I started to purr. Stephan took that as a sign that I was ready to play. He barreled into my side, dumping me unceremoniously into the cool waters. I splashed around, limbs everywhere in a desperate attempt to find land. He swam up, concerned for my safety.

I couldn't believe he'd bought that ruse. I dunked him, snorting with laughter at his expression. We played in the water, swimming, dunking each other, and just goofing off until the growls of our stomachs could no longer be ignored.

I hunted on our way back to the house, eating more than usual, as I knew he'd be opening my vein and consuming more blood than he normally did. We'd had a very long day, and I knew he was hungry. He was his usual patient self, waiting as I buried the remains of my food, never complaining or pushing me to do more than I was able to.

We arrived at the house. I filled his thermos, along with two other glasses I found in the house, with my blood. I went into the library and made it to the bay window before collapsing from utter exhaustion. I was out within minutes.

I woke to sunlight streaming in through the window. Sometime before he left, Stephan had placed a pillow under my head and a blanket over me. I must have really been out to not feel or remember him doing that.

"Natasha? I hoped you were awake. I brought you breakfast. Ham, eggs, and chocolate chip muffins." John smiled at me, his smile growing broader as my stomach growled with anticipation. I sniffed the air, searching for his unique scent underneath all the other delicious smells. I smiled when I found it.

"You know my weakness already: chocolate chip muffins. Where's Stephan?" I sat up, stretching the kinks from my back and reaching for the basket of food he held. He was quickly becoming one of my favorite people. Every time I saw him, he had food.

"He arrived at the club a few hours ago with instructions to help you with anything you may need. I arranged for a storage container to be brought in, as well as a large dumpster. They should arrive with the construction crew later this morning. Shall we get started with boxing things up?" I nodded, digging into the breakfast he'd brought.

"Weren't you supposed to help Marcy this week?" I was genuinely curious about this mysterious woman I'd heard mentioned but had yet to meet. John blushed.

"She doesn't really need any help with anything. Stephan said I could choose between the two, and this sounded like more fun." He wouldn't meet my eyes. I knew there was more to it, but he wasn't ready to share, and I wasn't about to pry. I just smiled, groaning as I bit into some ham. It was still warm. I changed the subject to something less personal.

"Do you know anything about auras? I meant to ask Stephan about it last night but got distracted." That seemed to happen more than I cared to admit. I still had so much to learn, but every time we started training, I lost track of everything but the joy and freedom of being an animal. I was so exhausted by the end of each night that I collapsed in the car on the way back to the club, questions forgotten. I also hadn't Dream-Walked since my first night here and was starting to think that was part of Stephan's plan. By the end of our training sessions, I was always too tired to concentrate on anything but his agenda. He wanted me to be as comfortable with changing as I was being human. I had to put my foot down and make him teach me about things other than changing. I was comfortable with it already. I enjoyed it even, but there was too much about being an Atlantean that I was ignorant about.

"I don't know much, I'm afraid. I know that your aura's pull is overwhelming to most humans. It's my understanding that it's stronger with the opposite sex, sort of a way to help increase procreation or help find your next meal, but I'm not sure exactly how it works. I know you can tone it down, but I have no idea how you manage that. Stephan doesn't give us the same training that he does with new vamps. Come to think of it, Stephan's never trained a new vamp before. Victoria was the closest to a trainee that he's ever had, but she was around before I was born. We, his servants, just have to know the basics so that we can assist you with your daily needs." He shrugged apologetically.

"I tried to tone it down yesterday, but it was really draining. That was part of the reason I was so irritated with your brother. I'd hoped there was a secret to it and that I was doing something wrong. I guess I'll have to remember to ask Stephan later. You're going to have to talk to everyone today while I hide." I grinned at him. "Either that, or you better have a large supply of hams available."

He laughed with me. Together, we started boxing up the library. I wanted to save all the books. Some were so old; they were handwritten originals. I had no idea how they were still in such good condition. When the guys dropped off the containers, John talked to them while I started loading boxes. It was nice to be super strong for once.

We went through every room in the house, methodically tossing and keeping various items. All the curtains were trashed, along with the mattresses, chamber pots, and furniture that'd been destroyed from melted wax or years of neglect. We kept the paintings. We were able to salvage most of the furniture and the little knickknacks scattered about the house. I wasn't sure if I wanted to keep them, but the pained look on John's face when he saw them convinced me that Stephan needed them.

While we cleaned out the house, the builders came and started tearing everything apart. They started in the foyer and continued around the house, following us as we emptied rooms. By dinner, the entire first floor looked less like a house and more like Swiss cheese. The windows were gone, the inside walls were stripped open, and the ceilings were gutted.

The storage container was packed, and the dumpster was filled. We'd have to order another one before the week was out. I was bushed with the amount of work we'd done, as well as the effort it took me to contain my aura during the few times I had to interact with the crew. I collapsed on the front lawn, sweating from the exertion of the day. John lay a few feet from me, panting.

"Oh, by the gods, kill me! I should've known better than to try and keep up with you." He groaned, smiling over at me. I grinned back.

"If it makes you feel any better, I'm impressed." As we were laughing, Stephan arrived with pizza. John and I could've kissed him. We devoured the pies, filling our bellies until they ached as badly as the rest of us. Stephan laughed at us, teasing us for acting like a bunch of frat boys before driving us back to the club to pass out.

The rest of the week was spent in a similar fashion. John and I would get up, go shopping, help with the renovations when we could, clean the house as best we could, and work on the gardens. Each evening, Stephan greeted us with a meal fit for a house full of people, and we'd talk about how things were going both in the club and a bit about the house. I always insisted on eating outside. I wanted to surprise Stephan when it was finished. It was easygoing, relaxing, and brought peaceful hope to my weary spirit. For the first time since changing, I could see a future for myself, a future that had me doing more than just waiting for Raif. I had hope.

By the end of the first week, the electrical and plumbing were all set, the windows were replaced, and I had the beginnings of a garage. I couldn't believe how quickly everything was going. I also started to stay at the house alone for longer periods. Stephan had a harder time adjusting to this than I did, something I found very strange and endearing.

The workers had left for the day, and I sent John home early so I could enjoy the peaceful tranquility of silence. I'd never realized before how loud construction workers really were until they left. Not only was there the banging and grinding of tools and equipment, but they also shouted at each other and blared music. I looked forward to the part of the day when I could enjoy the serenity of my home, alone.

I still couldn't believe this was mine. I walked around the perimeter, gauging how much work still needed to be done, and smiled. It was coming along beautifully, and I knew Stephan would be pleased at what I'd decided to do. I wanted everything to stay as it was, just upgraded. I had to rearrange some of the six bedrooms to create bathrooms, add indoor plumbing, and a septic system. I added electrical, upgraded the windows, and still had to repaint everything, but it was starting to look habitable.

I stopped abruptly as I walked back to the gardens. The birds were silent, their songs no longer a soothing chatter in the woods. I scented the air, curious about the disturbance. The birds had been quiet one other time, and that was when I'd inherited the house. The wildlife had gotten accustomed to Stephan and I roaming around the forest, even maintaining their nightly activities as we played. They were only quiet for newcomers. If you paid attention, the birds were better watchdogs than actual dogs.

I bristled in annoyance and a little fear. Stephan would be here soon, and I assumed he'd forgotten to tell me he was expecting company again. It would just be another in the long list of things he'd forgotten to tell me lately. I sighed, inhaling the unfamiliar scents as I did. Three Atlanteans were in my driveway.

I tried to relax, to keep my need to flee at bay. Stephan assured me this place was safe. No one that meant me harm knew this house existed. They had to be his friends and probably just wanted to meet me before anyone else, like Sonja.

I was apparently a big deal in the Atlantean community, although I was still having trouble accepting it. I knew I was instrumental in bringing their homeland back from the depths of the ocean where it had been hidden for over eleven thousand years, but I just didn't know what the big deal was. I couldn't figure out why some, like Stephan, were amazed by me, while others wanted me eliminated, like Stuart had. The wheels of change had already been set in motion. There wasn't anything else to do but wait. I'd already accomplished everything that needed to be done according to their stupid, ancient prophecy, but Stephan insisted that I still had to be careful around strangers.

I turned around, stuffing my apprehension down so I could meet the three Atlanteans properly. Stupidly, I wished I'd taken John up on his offer to stay with me. There wasn't anything a human could do against an Atlantean, but his company would've been nice.

I walked around to the front of the house just as they were starting up the steps. I relaxed immediately when I saw the woman. It was stupid and sexist of me, but I took comfort in her presence. She turned at my approach, smiling in greeting. She was stunning. Easily six feet, five inches. Her blond hair was braided in pigtails, and she had legs that went on forever. She had on low-slung jeans that looked expensive, a baby doll tee that was cut to show her abs, and sandals that were so gaudy I knew they cost more than all the shoes I owned.

The two men with her stayed a step behind as to remain unobtrusive but still protective of the woman. They wore only low-slung jeans that accented their toned bodies. Both were taller than the woman and almost matched Raif's bulk. They looked like twins with their matching shaved heads, wraparound sunglasses, and mirror image tattoos.

I felt like a complete country bumpkin with my hair in a messy ponytail, grubby shirt, and overalls. I smiled back at her, hoping I didn't have dirt on my face and silently cursing them all for arriving unannounced. They stopped in unison about six feet from me.

"You must be Natasha. Well, don't that just beat all? You're pint-sized! I'm Marie, and I just wanna say, it's a pleasure to finally meet you." She had the perfect southern drawl, complete with dimples and bubbly affect. I relaxed even further.

"Nice to meet you, Marie." I smiled up at her.

"These are my brothers, Tommy and Ben. We heard you were in town and just had to see what the fuss was about." Tommy and Ben each nodded in turn at their introduction. I nodded back to be polite. As friendly as they were, I still didn't feel comfortable having them here while I was alone.

"Stephan should be here soon. I'd invite you in, but everything is still torn apart."

"I guess we'd better hurry, then. We wouldn't want to hurt Stephan now, would we boys?" She raised her hands, and my feet sank in the dirt. Her brothers walked toward me, Tommy with a look of resignation, Ben with a gleeful smile. I panicked and tried to change. As I started to feel the trickle of transformation, a large fist came into my view. Everything went dark.

11

I came to in the back of a car. My hands were tied in front of me, and I was sandwiched between the two men.

"I wouldn't advise a repeat of your little stunt back there. Ben has no problem with knocking you unconscious again." Marie's voice was harsh. She was in the driver's seat, winding through the dark streets like a bat out of hell. The entire right side of my face was throbbing with the slow beat of my heart.

"Where are you taking me?" My voice was stronger than I felt.

"To Nicholas." It was all she'd say for the remainder of the ride. I tried to pay attention to each turn we made so I could find my way back. Trouble was, I didn't know how long I'd been out, and I could barely focus past the pain and dizziness in my head.

All I could discern from brief glances out the tinted windows were dark forms of trees. We were still surrounded by the forest, and therefore still had to be in the Everglades. That was no help, the glades covered over eight hundred miles.

The sharp turns Marie was making in her small car were starting to make me nauseous. My head throbbed behind my eyes, adding to the nauseated feel. I had a nagging suspicion that had I been anything other than Atlantean, the blow I'd received would have killed me. Spots of light danced in my vision, and I thought I was on the verge of passing out again. My stomach lurched, and I closed my eyes for a second to clear my vision.

When I opened them, the spots remained. I groaned. I blinked my eyes rapidly, hoping that would clear the lights and I wouldn't get sick. They remained. It took me a minute to focus and realize that the spots weren't in my head; they were getting brighter. The trees parted, revealing a massive old plantation, lit to be a beacon for the blind.

"Natasha, know that this is just business. You can't help who you are any more than I can help who I am. Just do yourself a favor and do whatever Nicholas asks. You may eventually walk out of here if you do." Marie met my eyes briefly in the mirror, and for a split second, I saw remorse. It was quickly covered by a slight nod of her head, followed by a sharp bite to my side, jolting my entire body. It was the worst pain I'd ever experienced in my life. I blacked out for the second time that night.

I woke slowly this time. My face still hurt, but it wasn't throbbing to the beat of my pulse anymore. I gave quick thanks for my new healing abilities and prayed I'd be finished with testing them. My side was tender, my throat was scratchy, and the taste of vomit was present in my mouth. I realized I was lying on a leather couch in some sort of office. I sat up slowly, allowing my head time to adjust to an elevated position. Leaning against the arm of the couch for support, I surveyed the dim room. A small lamp on a massive desk in front of the couch lit the area. A large, wide leather chair swiveled behind the desk to reveal an equally wide man.

"I was starting to wonder when you'd come around. I sincerely apologize for your treatment thus far. Marie assured me it was absolutely necessary to render you unconscious. I hope you weren't harmed too badly. My healer had a look at you and declared you healthy enough. She said it would just be a matter of time before you regained consciousness. I'm pleased to see she wasn't mistaken.

"Allow me to introduce myself. I am Nicholas. When we're through, I'm certain that you and I shall be the greatest of friends." His smile made me shudder. It was a smile that held perverted satisfaction, filled with confidence and knowledge of things I prayed I'd never know. He appeared to be short, probably not much taller than myself, but wide. He had the tanned skin of someone from the tropics, close cropped hair, and a nicely trimmed goatee. He was unassuming and somewhat attractive, if you ignored the creepy smile.

"What do you want with me?" I croaked out.

"I want to liberate you from your bond. I want to return you to the life that was cruelly taken from you." He handed me a glass of water and two pills. "It's water and aspirin. If you wish, I can have Maurice bring some food to your room later."

"You mean you're not going to kill me?" I didn't trust him. I sniffed the aspirin, recognizing the familiar chemical compounds, and took them with the cool water. It felt like heaven on my abused throat. He waited until I'd taken the pills to continue speaking, with a look of pained shock that would have impressed anyone in theatre.

"Of course not, my dear! I simply wish for things to remain as they are. Having Atlantis rise would be catastrophic. If we succeed in removing the bonds you have with your mate, we can prevent the prophesy from ever coming to fruition. This would prevent Atlantis from rising, prevent humans from knowing the existence of creatures they relegated to fiction, and prevent a war that would end all life on this planet. Can you not see the effects your actions would have on the masses? Your mate desired you, selfishly. Imagine what that selfish act could do to the rest of civilization. It would be devastating. I simply wish to prevent war."

"You're too late. I've already given my tears, mated, and left Atlantis. The prophecy's been fulfilled. It's just a matter of time until Atlantis rises, and your people join the rest of civilization." I spoke with certainty, but inwardly, I could almost see his point of view. I'd never even considered how humans would react with knowing that supernatural beings really did walk among them. I had to believe that humans would eventually come to accept the Atlantean people. Above all else, I had to hope. He looked at me with confusion and pity.

"You mean you truly don't know?"

"Know what?" He looked at me with such pity, I almost felt as if he truly cared about me. For a brief second, I felt his remorse for kidnapping me, having me beaten, and now for telling me something that would cause me grief. Then I remembered that he had me kidnapped and beaten into unconsciousness—twice. This man could not be trusted.

"It truly pains me to be the one to burden you with this knowledge. It was not my intention to cause you grief. I fear you were not told everything when you were mated. The entire prophecy goes like this: 'A lesson must be learned for gods and men to live in harmony. Atlantis shall descend to be hidden from gods and men. Until the time the soul mates and willingly chooses to break, you shall be apart from your heart. Atlantis will join the ranks again when tears are freely given. Death created devastation; death shall be your preservation.'" He paused for effect. "Do you understand what that means?" I shook my head. No. A terrible feeling started in my chest, squeezing my heart painfully. "I cannot believe no one has told you. That is even more cruel than forcing you to become the mate of an immortal. You and your mate have come closer to satisfying the demands of prophesy than any other mated pair in our history, but there is still one more thing that must be done. One more sacrifice to be made."

A chill crept over my skin. There were only two of us involved in the prophecy, Raif and me. I didn't want him to say it. I couldn't hear it, but I couldn't stop him either. My throat was dry, my heart thudding in my chest. I couldn't hear the lies my heart already believed.

"Your mate must become a willing sacrifice on Poseidon's altar. His blood must flow, coating the steps of the altar in penance for Atlas's betrayal of the gods. He must willingly die. Death created devastation; death shall be our preservation."

"No, you're wrong. He'd have told me. He said we'd be together again when Atlantis rose. He promised. You're lying!" I was shaking. I couldn't believe him—I wouldn't! There was no way Raif would mate with me, knowing it would cause his death. He wouldn't hide something that important from me; he couldn't.

"I'll give you until tomorrow to think about things. The only way to save your mate's life is to remove the bond that was created, to return you to your humanity. You would both live as you had before you met. Our two civilizations would continue in the peaceful ignorance they've had for centuries. Think about it." With that, he nodded to someone behind me and left the room. I turned to see who had entered the room without me noticing. Tommy—I could tell from his tattoos, which were opposite from his brother's—was leaning against the wall next to the door.

I shrank back in fear. I knew I shouldn't, that any sign of submissiveness I showed was a weakness, but after the abduction, he and his brother terrified me. His posture finally registered in my confused, terrified brain. He was leaning with shoulders turned away, his eyes downcast, and arms casually hanging by his side, palms open. He was doing his best to appear nonthreatening and submissive to me. I couldn't figure out why he'd want to do that after establishing that he was okay with abuse.

"Forgive me for what happened earlier. We were only supposed to ask you to join us, not cause you harm. Marie and Ben get carried away sometimes. Allow me to escort you to your room." He held the door open for me, keeping his eyes downcast. I would've been stupid to trust him, but I also knew I needed a place to think. I couldn't stay in Nicholas's office all night. Besides, they had to think I was at least willing to accept their proposal if I had any chance at escape or rescue.

He led me down a hall to a door on the left. There were doors lined on either side of the hall, all closed with no indication of stairs either up or down. From the windowless office to the monochromatic hallway, I had no idea where I was or how to escape. I did know that I had to try to figure these things out and figure out how to contact Stephan. Silently, I cursed him for not training me more in Dream-Walking.

Tommy opened the door, keeping his eyes lowered in submission. His demeanor didn't fool me. He'd already showed that he was comfortable with abuse and mild torture by not doing anything to stop his brother. The room itself was small, sparsely decorated, with a private bath. There were two small windows flanking the bed that had curtains covering them. I avoided looking at them too long, hoping that Tommy hadn't noted my excitement at a possible escape route.

"Don't bother changing. Nicholas placed a charm on you to prevent that from happening. There are armed guards both in the house and on the property for your safety and protection. The windows are electrified and alarmed. We're also five stories up, and while you'd survive that fall, it would hurt like hell and take time for the bones to heal." He recited the information like he was bored and did this all the time. For all I knew, kidnapping and torturing women was an everyday occurrence for him. My heart dropped at the mention of the electrified windows. I thought that was all, but he continued in a softer voice.

"Do yourself a favor, Natasha, just do what he says. Wouldn't it be nice to be able to go back to your old life? To be human again, and to know that by doing so, your mate would live?" He finally looked at me, and the pain in his eyes surprised me. Before I could answer, he bowed and walked out of the room.

I had to get out of here. No way was I allowing them to sever the bonds I had with Raif. I didn't believe he was supposed to die. I refused to. Bad guys always tell you things to scare you into doing what they want. It was bad guy rule number one. I just had to get out of here.

I started checking the windows. Sure enough, we were five stories up, and I could hear the hum of electricity next to my cheek. I swore softly, remembering the jolt in the car. I didn't even care if I would live through it; the threat of that pain was enough of a deterrent. I noticed the armed guards patrolling the compound. Some had lights, and some wore strange things on their heads. All were armed with huge guns.

I went to the bedroom door to see if I could try looking for the stairs. I didn't remember seeing anyone patrolling this floor, so maybe they were all outside. I opened the door, revealing Tommy on the other side. He was sitting sprawled out against the wall across from my door, settling in for a long night of boredom. He raised an eyebrow, and I quickly shut the door again. I really was trapped.

I sat on the bed. Doubt was creeping over me. I'd known for a while that Stephan was hiding something from me. What if it was the second half of the prophecy? I didn't want to believe that Stephan or Raif would hide something so huge from me.

I thought about returning to humanity, leaving all the craziness of Atlantis behind. It was very tempting. If there was one thing I'd gained from all of Stephan's trainings, though, it was a love for being a Changer. The freedom, the simple joy of running—it was all so intoxicating. I didn't think I could go back to being simply human, knowing what I knew now.

If Nicholas was telling the truth, Raif would die unless I allowed our bonds to be severed. For the first time, I allowed the thought to take root in my mind. If I allowed our bonds to be severed, Raif wouldn't have any reason to die. He could live and thrive as he had for centuries. I could finish out my meager existence on this planet knowing that when I died, he would still live a long and happy life.

Despite myself, I scoffed. Raif hadn't lived a happy life before we'd met. He'd simply existed. He was hated for his position, lonely and alone. His only friends were Michael and, strangely enough, Atreyu. Even if I did sever the bonds, when he left Cleito's protective castle, his people would kill him for deceiving them. If he stayed in her castle and Poseidon found out about me severing the bonds, I was certain he'd find a way to destroy us both in a fit of rage.

I had to get out of here. That was my only solution. I had to escape, find Stephan, and have him settle this. If Nicholas was telling the truth, and there really was a way to sever the bonds, Stephan would know. It would hurt beyond measure if Nicholas was right, but I had to hear it from Stephan before I'd allow myself to believe it. As of this moment, all I was certain of was that I absolutely had to get out of here.

I tried to change. I thought about being something small enough to blend in and hide from everyone: a mouse. I wasn't sure if I'd be able to pull off something so small, but I figured that if I could gain mass to be a large cat, I could theoretically lose mass to be a mouse. I felt the trickles of the change start, followed quickly by a sharp shooting pain from my ankle. It was bad enough that I cried out and stopped my transformation. Pulling my pant leg up, I found the charm Tommy had told me about. Around my ankle was a tiny cuff made of what looked like braded iron, silver, and copper with little emeralds and sapphires dangling from the braid. I couldn't find a clasp and wondered how such a small thing could prevent me from changing.

I radiated with anger. It was the final straw. First, they kidnapped me, then knocked me unconscious—twice. They imprisoned me in some room, and now they'd removed my ability to change. Apparently, this was the cost of finding your soul mate and wanting a life with him.

My anger reached its breaking point. I'd been hunted and attacked more since meeting Raif than I had in thirty years as a human—even a human doing questionable genetic research. I was pissed and scared, sick and tired of being left in the dark. If what Nicholas said was true, I didn't want to be a part of it. I didn't want to know this deep connection, only to have it be severed so that a race of people could continue to survive. We'd gotten along just fine for eleven thousand years. Atlantis could rot for all I cared.

I knew I didn't want to be a part of this culture anymore. Why in the world would Raif want to liberate these people, to add unstable Atlanteans into the human population? I knew what I had to do, what needed to be done. My decision was firm, doubt completely obliterated from my soul at the sight of that tiny little anklet.

I did the only thing I could after that. I bathed and went to bed. I tried to search out Stephan in my dreams, to tell him what was happening and how to find me. Certainly, if I could Dream-Walk to him, he could guide things from there. I wasn't sure if my captors knew I was a Walker, but since they were allowing me to sleep, I figured it was still a secret. I tried my best to contact Stephan, giving myself a splitting headache as I concentrated. Nothing happened. I couldn't find him, couldn't find Raif. Hell, I didn't dream at all. I tossed and turned on the bed until Tommy came to get me the next day.

12

It was close to noon when Tommy walked into my room carrying a small tray of food. After what Stephan had been providing me the past couple of weeks, this was pitiful. My stomach growled loudly, reminding me that I hadn't eaten since noon the day prior. I was starving and tired from my restless sleep.

I thanked Tommy for the food. Somehow knowing I wouldn't be offered more, I desperately tried to pace myself and not look like a ravenous animal. If they were trying to treat me like a guest, they really should have taken a lesson from Stephan on how to properly feed a Changer. I was hungrier after the small meal than I was before I started. Maybe starvation was a part of the process of breaking my bond with Raif, and Nicholas had decided to eliminate that decision from me as well.

When I was finished, I followed a silent Tommy out of the room. He led me down the hall in the same direction we came from last night. It was as monochromatic during the day as it was at night. I had no idea how he knew what door to pick. It seemed as if he opened one at random and walked through, expecting me to follow. I caught a glimpse of stairs below, so I hurried to keep up. It appeared he was taking me closer to the ground floor.

Each floor was the same as the one before it. We'd go down one flight of stairs, open the door to a hall of doors, go through another one, and repeat the process until we reached the ground floor. I was tingling with anticipation. All I had to do now was find the front door and make a break for it. The front door would have to be different from all the rest; front doors were always different from interior doors. Tommy opened the door to the first floor, and my heart stuttered. The floor was identical to all the others.

He led me farther down the hall this time, going almost to the last door before deciding to open one on our right. Behind this door was a decently sized library filled with books, a large cherry wood desk, and large, soft-looking chairs. Nicholas was sitting behind the desk, clicking away on a laptop. He barely glanced my way as Tommy directed me to have a seat. My giddy feeling immediately disappeared, leaving only a hollow pit of unease nagging at my psyche.

"Good morning, Natasha. I trust you slept well." He was perky and full of cheer as he lowered the lid to his computer.

"Actually, it was awful. This thing on my ankle itches. Would you mind taking it off?" I tried not to snip. I coated my words in honey. I tried to ignore my irritation, anger, and hunger to imitate his good cheer, to show him I could be reasonable and kind, just like him. It didn't work.

"I am terribly sorry for the discomfort, unfortunately we must maintain our safe practices for both you and us, at least until you finish the cleansing process. Have you come to a decision?" The cleansing process. That was a cute term for separating Raif and me forever.

"Yes, I have. Remove this thing and I'll tell you." I could be stubborn, too.

"Natasha, what guarantees do I have of you not changing into some horrible beast and murdering all of my people that I so dearly care for? Everyone here relies on me to keep them safe, to protect them from the danger other Atlanteans pose to them. If I were to release you, without a guarantee of their safety, I would lose my reputation and my followers. Certainly, you can understand how the poor humans would feel if I let you loose to snack on them?"

"I wouldn't eat a person if they were the last thing available. That's disgusting. I give you my word. Until I'm off your property, I won't Change. That should be acceptable. I've shown myself to be agreeable to things so far. Besides, you have Tommy right there. If I start to do something you don't like, he'll just knock me out again and solve your problem for you." I smiled politely back. I wanted this thing off.

I knew it was the reason I wasn't able to Dream-Walk, and I knew that was going to be my only way out of here. I had to contact Stephan. They weren't going to let me simply walk away. I had to hope that whatever they were going to do to me would wait until tomorrow and I'd be given a night without this anklet to try and reach Stephan.

Nicholas stared at me for a long while, considering his options. I knew he wasn't certain if I'd be a willing subject in his avenues of torture or not, and for some reason, he wanted me compliant. What better way than to show me he could be reasonable than to remove the anklet? It still surprised me when he nodded.

He came around the desk and bent toward my foot. I had to repress a shudder at his touch. Gently, he held the braid, whispering words I couldn't understand under his breath as it stretched so he could guide it off my foot.

"Thank you," I whispered. He went back to the comfort of his desk, folding his hands in a steeple on the mahogany surface. I resisted the urge to wipe my ankle now that it was free.

"Now, are you going back to your old life, or continuing with the torment of this one?"

"Before I answer, I have a few questions." He raised an eyebrow at my boldness, and I persisted. His answers wouldn't change my mind, but I still wanted to know. "Have you ever done this before, how many times, and how successful was it?" I didn't ask if it hurt. I had a feeling I already knew that answer.

"Yes, we've attempted this procedure in order to be assured of its integrity." He stuttered ever so slightly. "Every test has been successful." He smoothed his thick fingers on the desk. Smiling benignly at me, he looked the part of the concerned citizen. I knew he was lying, but not certain as to which part he was lying about. I didn't have any other way to delay the inevitable. With a pounding heart, I spoke.

"I want to stay as I am. I chose to become mated. It wasn't forced on me. Even if you're right, Atlantis deserves to be in its proper position. My mate made the decision, knowing full well what it entailed. If he was agreeable to it, then I have to accept his decision. I appreciate your offer, but I would like to stay as I am." I stood on shaking legs, ready to leave. If he really wanted me to believe I had a choice in the matter, he'd let me walk out the door. We both knew he wouldn't.

"Perhaps this will change your mind." He reached below the desk and did something. One of the panels on the library wall slid to the side revealing a staircase that led down. I looked toward the staircase with trepidation. All I could see past the entryway was darkness.

Out of the dark, I heard a painful groan. It sent shivers down my spine. The little hairs on the nape of my neck stood on end. I didn't want to see what was in the darkness. I didn't want to, but I knew I had to. My conscience wouldn't let me ignore the small whimpers of pain I could hear coming out of the darkness.

"Come, my dear." Nicholas walked around his desk and held his hand out toward me. Tommy was a warm presence behind, eliminating any illusion of choice that I had. My throat was dry as I stepped forward. Ignoring Nicholas's outstretched hand, I walked into the darkness.

My nose was assaulted first with smells that reminded my belly that I hadn't eaten adequately in a while. Knowing that the blood, fresh meat, and bone-jarring terror that permeated the room were caused from torturing someone I knew halted the grumbling of my stomach. The scents got thicker as we walked farther down the stairs, deeper into the black abyss beyond.

Involuntarily, I inhaled deeply. For a split second, I enjoyed the way the scents tickled across my pallet; the thick, coppery scent of blood had me salivating. Once I got past the dinner smells of the tortured human, my mouth dried, and a growl echoed across the room. Underneath the raw meat was a faint scent that I would recognize anywhere. I'd smelled it every year of my life before leaving Nevada—the clearing of the summer fires to release the sweet scent of sagebrush in the fall. It was John.

My steps faltered with the realization that they'd tortured John for my benefit. I couldn't stop growling. I didn't want to see what they'd done to him; the smell was bad enough. I glanced over at Nicholas. Through the dim light, I could barely make out his serene expression. I wanted to kill him in that moment. I'd never taken such immense pleasure in visualizing the brutal death of another person before.

Deep into the cavern, someone was lighting torches. I wasn't certain if that was due to lack of electricity, or if it helped with the creepy ambiance of Nicholas's torture chamber. Either way, I was thoroughly unnerved. In between the lit torches, I could see various weapons. I couldn't even imagine what some of them were used for. I shivered as I heard John moan again.

In the middle of the room, now fully illuminated by the torchlight, was a large slab table with a naked man strapped to it. John was completely covered in cuts, bruises, and blood. I ran to his side only to be stopped by Tommy.

"That's quite close enough, my dear. Would you like to reconsider your decision, or do you need further persuasion?" Nicholas smiled at me, full of virtue and excitement. I knew he wanted me to give him a reason to inflict pain onto John. I wouldn't give him one.

"Please, just heal him and let him go. I'll do anything you want." I wouldn't look at Nicholas. I forced myself to stare at the mess they'd made of John. I wanted to remember what they did to him and inflict every cut, every bruise, and every amount of torture onto Nicholas when I escaped.

I would escape here, and he would know my wrath.

"Very well. I knew we could come to an agreement. Tommy, help our guest to Madelyn's room. Natasha, if you would follow me." As Tommy picked John up to carry him away, I heard him whispering something.

"Wait, please." I walked over and gently touched John's cheek. He winced. "I am so sorry they did this to you." John's voice came out strangled, hoarse from screaming so much. I had to lean very close to hear him.

"Remember that which makes you special," he whispered, coughing and groaning in agony when he was finished. My face was splattered with his blood. Nicholas better pray I die. If I didn't, I vowed then and there to make him suffer for this.

Nicholas led me through a passage hidden in the depths of the cavernous room, wisely not trying to touch me. I followed, hoping John would live and be able to tell Stephan how to find us. I didn't know what Nicholas had planned for me, but I knew it wouldn't be good.

The passage led to another dark cavern, this one with electricity. A single bulb illuminated a large round tank of water. Ben hovered excitedly next to it.

"Please remove your clothing and climb onto the tank."

I hesitated for just a moment before following Nicholas's instructions. Naked, I climbed the ladder on the side of the enclosed tank and saw that there was a hinged opening, just large enough for a person to slide into. It reminded me of the old magician's water trick.

"Climb into the tank." Nicholas hadn't moved from his position near the entrance to this cavern. He cleared his throat. The tank started to jostle as someone else climbed the ladder. I took a breath and slid into the water just as Ben's head cleared the top of the ladder.

My heart was pounding in the tepid water. I couldn't see anything from inside the tank, but I could hear as Ben closed the lid behind me. I panicked. Kicking to the surface, I tried desperately to push open the hatch, to no avail. I launched myself from the bottom and hit the hatch with my shoulder. Nothing happened. I clawed at it, desperation clouding my mind as my lungs screamed in agony.

He meant to kill me. I was going to drown here, naked, in a crazy man's water tank. My last thought before I gasped in a mouthful of water was that I was glad Raif would at least live. I didn't choke. I gulped in the water and didn't choke. Numbly, I attempted to breathe. I could breathe under water! I smiled at this miracle—I could breathe. Vaguely, I remembered hearing Stephan's voice telling me we were descended from a water deity and that we all had an affinity with that element to a certain extent.

I was so relieved, I swam in circles for a while, enjoying the fact that I was alive and breathing under water. I thought about Nicholas, and my swimming slowed. I had no idea what his intentions were with me, or why he placed me in a vat of water, but

I knew it couldn't be good. I still had to figure out how to get out of here, how to escape. I had to try to Dream without alerting Nicholas to what I was doing.

I swam up to the side of the tank and peered out as best I could. I couldn't see anything. Shrugging, I swam far away from where I'd last seen Nicholas and curled down on the bottom of the tank. My back was facing the spot I thought he was, and I closed my eyes, knowing there wasn't anything else I could do to hide myself. I would just have to hope for the best. I didn't think I'd be able to sleep, let alone find Stephan in my dreams, but they sucked me under almost immediately.

I was in a strange room filled with candles and thick, pungent smoke. It was a place I'd never seen, but it felt important. I looked around for a familiar face and was sad when I couldn't find one. Out of the fog, I heard a voice that made me smile and want to weep at the same time.

"Natasha? Are you there?" Stephan sounded hopeful and hesitant at the same time. I hoped he could hear me too.

"Stephan? Where are you?" The relief in my voice was palpable. I looked around for him again. This time, I saw his shade wading through the fog. I ran toward him, jumping into his arms. I didn't even think as I held him close to me. His arms instantly went around my body, clutching me close to him as if he could bring me back to him through our conjoined dream.

"Thank Poseidon I found you! I've been looking for you but kept getting blocked. I can't sense anything beyond trees. Where are you?" He leaned back to talk to me.

I could see the relief etched in his magnesium eyes and gave in. It was only a dream after all. I fisted my hands in his long black hair and kissed him as if my world would end without him. At this moment, I fully believed it would. He kissed me back without hesitation. There weren't any thoughts of Raif as I clutched Stephan to me—only this man who'd come to mean more to me than I was willing to admit.

We stood, locked in an embrace for eternity, our lips conveying in this dream state what would never be stated aloud. I didn't want to let him go, but knew I had to tell him what I came here to say. I didn't know if I'd get another chance. I was almost certain I wouldn't. I had to get out of here.

"Nicholas is trying to break the mating bonds and return me to my human state," I said breathlessly as I pulled away. He dropped me. My unsteady legs wouldn't support me, and I collapsed onto the floor.

"He's doing what?" he asked as he lifted me off the floor.

"I'm in the basement of this huge house being cleansed of my mating bonds. He has John." It was getting more and more difficult to speak. I tried clearing my throat. My head and lungs hurt.

"What's with this fog? I'm having a hard time breathing." He went pale, which was a trick for him. I coughed again, this time spitting out water.

"What is he doing? Never mind. I will be there as soon as I can. Stay alive for me, Tasha. I want you to close your eyes and think of the place you left. You have to get back and live. Fight!" He crushed me to him one last time.

I saw the fear briefly in his eyes and could feel him trembling as he crushed his mouth desperately against mine. I kissed him with the same fervor. If I was honest in any moment, it was now, in our dream, with the knowledge that this may be the last we saw of each other.

I woke up choking and coughing up water, still in the tank. I swam up to the hatch to try and open it. It was still sealed tight against me. This time I knew I really was drowning. I clutched at my throat, gagging on the water that had been so wonderful just hours before. My vision went spotty at the edges, and I knew I was dying. Everything went dark seconds before I heard the lock on the hatch disengage.

Someone splashed into the water with me. Large hands lifted me up and out of the tank. I fell to the ground like a sack of potatoes. Seconds later, I was lifted and slung over a broad shoulder. I was carried into another area and flopped back onto the ground. I started coughing up water. My whole body shook. It was dark and cold, and I just wanted to go home.

Light exploded behind my closed eyelids. I scrunched them tighter and curled into a ball. It got very hot, very quickly, and I slowly opened my eyes. I bolted upright. The entire room was engulfed in flames. They inched their way closer to me as if they had a purpose and a mind of their own. I scooted closer to the corner of the wall until there wasn't any room left to run. The flames followed. They filled the room, rushing toward me as if their only purpose in life was to dance along my skin.

I curled into myself, protecting my body as best I could with my arms and legs. The flames caught hold of my hair, singeing it to the root. As the flames licked against my body, I screamed. I leapt up and darted around the room, searching for a spot that wasn't engulfed in flame. I screamed until I couldn't scream anymore. My throat burned from the inside out. There wasn't a spot on my body that wasn't red or blistered. I fell to the ground, finally giving in to the flames. My body tried to heal me as quickly as the skin was being destroyed, and I was in agony, whimpering as the flames continued to roast me alive until I blessedly blacked out from the pain.

I woke again in agonizing pain. Something was scratching my already ruined skin. I tried to move my arms, succeeding only in dumping dirt on my face. I stopped moving. I tried not to panic as I realized I'd now been buried alive.

I knew I couldn't be too far down. Nicholas would have to be able to monitor me to make sure I didn't die on him. At this point, it was clear to me he didn't want me dead. As it was, I didn't know how much air I had left. I didn't know how deep I was buried or how long I'd been here. The only thing I knew for certain was I hurt, and I needed to escape. Now.

I took the biggest breath I could, wincing as the movements tore open my healing skin, and started to dig my way out of my grave. I dug until my lungs felt like bursting. Ignoring the pain covering my body, I dug. Cupping my hands around my face, I took another breath. I had to do this twice more before I felt air on my fingers. I dug frantically for an opening I could crawl out of, eating dirt as I did so.

I coughed, spitting out clods of blood-soaked dirt as I emerged from the earth. I wanted to open my eyes to see where I was so I could run, but I couldn't move. Instead, I lay atop my almost grave and sucked in deep breaths of air.

It was very quiet; the only sound was that of my breathing. Slowly, I tried opening my eyes. They hurt, too. I didn't think there was a spot on my body that didn't hurt. I blinked a few times to get my vision to adjust. When the haze finally cleared, I discovered that I was in a clearing in the woods. It was the exact place I wanted to be. If I could, I'd have wept with joy in that moment.

I managed to stand up, moving slowly. I picked a direction and started walking. Each step pulled and cracked my skin, leaving rivulets of blood in my wake. I forced myself past the pain and continued. Each step was a step toward freedom.

I made it to the woods surrounding the clearing when lights shone and wind pummeled me from every direction. The moist air was a balm on my skin for a split second. The wind kicked up, knocking me to my knees and flinging small rocks, sticks, and other debris around. I curled into myself, protecting my stomach and groaning in pain and frustration. Where was Stephan?

I stayed like that until the wind died down. Dirt, grass, and twigs were stuck to the healing blisters on my skin. I didn't have the energy to move, let alone change and run away. Besides, I couldn't leave John. I had to wait until Stephan came to rescue us. I wouldn't risk John's life just to end my suffering. I wouldn't leave without him.

I heard voices moments before I was lifted into one of the twin's massive arms. He winced at my crusted form and held me as gently as possible. I had to be in Tommy's arms, and I silently thanked him for being the one to offer me shelter. It was pointless for him to be gentle, though. There wasn't a spot on my body that wasn't in agony. Every movement hurt. I couldn't see past the fog of my vision to where he was taking me, but I could hear the sound of his steps change as he entered a cavernous room. He was leading me back inside. I whimpered.

"I'm so sorry, Natasha. I had no idea what he wanted with you. Had I known this was what would happen, I never would've let them take you. Please, don't struggle. If I can, I'll find a way to get you out of here," he whispered and held me tighter to him.

"John. Where's John?" My voice couldn't even be considered a voice any longer. It came out as a croaked, scratchy whisper that tore the lining of my throat with that small question.

"He's healing. Madelyn's a good healer, even though she's with Nicholas. He'll be healed completely in a few days, and I will personally escort him back to Stephan's. Just hang on until then, and I promise I'll find a way to rescue you as well. This was so wrong. I'm so sorry, Natasha." His voice broke with unshed tears.

I was surprised to feel gratitude toward Tommy. I didn't think any of my captors could show compassion, let alone want to help me. He was different from our first encounter, and I was glad for that. I wanted to tell him I forgave him, that it wasn't his fault, but couldn't form the words. I had a glimmer of hope that things would be okay. I just had to survive the cleansing process.

"You'll feel better in a few minutes. It isn't the healing waters of Atlantis, but Poseidon works wonders with any body of water, and I know he'll heal you now. The longer you can stay in the water, the better off you'll be. Stay strong."

He gently carried me into a pool of sulfuric healing water. I sighed as he wiped my blistered skin clean with the pungent water. He lightly drizzled water on my face, moistening my abused eyes. I could feel myself healing. It was exhausting. I was too tired to pull away from him, content to simply not feel pain for the moment.

I dozed briefly, waking to the rumbling of my stomach. How I could be hungry after enduring so much pain was beyond me. I was also acutely aware that the man who held me wasn't clothed. He appeared to be extremely happy to be holding my naked, healing body.

"Feeling better?" Tommy asked, nuzzling my neck with his nose. His breath sent involuntary shivers down my body, hardening my nipples and moistening my core. I cringed at my body's reaction, praying he'd ignore it and let me go.

"Yes, thank you. Is it over now?" My throat was killing me. I still couldn't completely focus my vision on anything, but my body was no longer screaming in agony.

"I'm afraid not. Nicholas will continue to use the elements to cleanse you of your physical bonds. Once those are removed,

Madelyn is to heal your body and rid you of your spiritual bonds."
His husky voice rasped against my chin.

One of his arms tightened reflexively around my waist while
the other continued to bathe me in the healing waters. His arousal
continued to bob against my hip, belying his earlier insistence that
he didn't want to be a part of this. As hard as I tried to ignore it, it
bothered me. I squirmed to escape his embrace.

"You are so beautiful," he whispered against my throat,
turning his head to nuzzle behind my ear. "How could you still be
so loyal to a man who obviously doesn't want you?"

"W-what?" I whispered, still raw from the abuse of the
elements.

"Raifuku used you. You're only a means to an end for him.
You know that, right?" Tommy's eyes bored into mine, begging me
to believe him. "Raifuku's only desire has been to be reunited with
my sister. They knew each other as younglings and promised to
mate when they were of age. Marie was devastated when Atlantis
sank."

His words shattered my heart. Why would Raif want me,
when he had Marie? No wonder he was in such a hurry to get me
out of Atlantis. The faster the prophecy was completed, the faster
he could be reunited with the person he actually loved. Something
didn't sit right with Tommy's words though.

"Why sever the bonds then?" I croaked, pain and heartbreak
lacing my words.

"An Atlantean has to die, not a human convert, and Marie
would like to have her fiancé." His words made sense. "There will
be another mated pair. They will fulfill the prophecy, and then she
and Raifuku can be together again. Once he sees that she waited for
him, he'll discard you in a heartbeat. You're just a means to an end
for him."

"Why?" I asked, the pain in my voice alerting him to the full
question. *Why are you telling me this?*

"I would never do that to you," he whispered against my ear.
"I would show you such love and devotion, you would never think
the name Raifuku again. I can see your beauty." His hands roamed
freely across my body, leaving my nerve endings on edge. "I would

never abandon you. Never use you. I would only show you pleasure beyond comprehension." He did just as he said, using his fingers to ease an ache I'd had since I left Atlantis.

"I would show you the true joys of being a Changer. I wouldn't leave you to have to learn from a vampire." He spoke the words with such disgust, as if the thought of leaving me alone was abhorrent.

A part of me craved him—at least, craved what he was offering. A place to be welcomed, loved, cherished—a true soul mate. As the doubt and confusion settled in, he gently carried me to the tank.

"No," I protested, squirming in his slick embrace.

"We must remove your bonds to the one who wants to use you if we're to be together. Don't you want to be loved?" He nuzzled against my cheek.

I did. I wanted love more than anything.

13

I drowned, was burned, buried, and battered by the wind so often it was becoming my routine. I didn't know how long I was there—days, hours, or months. Time no longer mattered to me. I'd lost hope of escape or survival around the fourth time Tommy carried me back from being battered by the wind. I was weak, starving, and in constant agony. I prayed for death.

Each time I saw him; I asked about John. Each time, his answer was the same. He was healing with Madelyn, and once he was strong enough, they'd find a way to get me out of this hell. I couldn't let go of the flicker of hope that John was alive, that he'd at least find refuge with Stephan. I begged to see him for myself, to see with my own eyes that he was healing.

Tommy had finished cleaning me as I hung limp and lifeless against the side of the hot spring. His constant stories of Raif and Marie ate away any hope I had that I'd truly found my soul mate. Doubt clouded my brain, removing any ounce of hope I'd ever had at finding love in Raif's arms again. Pain was my constant state of being. I couldn't remember a time when I didn't hurt.

Tommy's gentleness was my only refuge. He showed he cared, giving constantly, only asking that I be strong, so we would be free to be together. I didn't even know if that was what I wanted. I just wanted the agony of this to end. I was starting to feel some affection toward him though; each time I found myself in his embrace, I relaxed further into accepting him and his lust for me.

"Nicholas said I could take you to see John today if you're able to walk on your own." His hand trailed up and down my back with gentle strokes. I couldn't muster the energy to care, but I knew I had to see that John was okay, if only so this torment could end. I

114

did feel a flicker of some emotion other than pain at the mention of Nicholas's name and tried to grasp it. It fluttered away as elusive as hope.

I broke out in a sweat as I tried to stand. It was the first time I'd attempted to move since my first cleansing. It took more effort than I expected. I was extremely weak. My voice sounded odd to my ears—scratchy, thin, and without inflection.

"Take me to him."

Tommy led me up one flight of stairs, out into the hall, and through a door on my right. I was still naked, my abused skin too sensitive to handle clothing of any kind. I didn't care. I just wanted to see that John was okay.

He lay in the middle of a massive bed, lights low to protect his eyes from their glare. I sank to my knees in relief when his eyes opened and looked at me.

"Natasha? What have they done to you?" His voice was a blend of horror and surprise. He leapt out of bed and came close to me. He paled as he looked at my abraded body. He looked perfect.

I don't know what it was that made me scent him. Either mistrust at the tiny flicker of hope furled in the hollow excuse of my heart, or the knowledge that Nicholas couldn't be trusted. Either way, I lifted my nose to him as he came closer and searched for the familiar scent of sagebrush in the fall. It was missing.

My hands curled into fists, nails elongating and biting into my palms. A small part of me that could still function realized two things in that moment. First, this wasn't John. Second, this was the reason John and I were both here.

"It was you," I rasped, the accusation causing James to pale even further. He'd led the siblings to my home to abduct me. Rage blossomed in my chest. I could barely speak past the rage that burned inside me. "Not John."

"What? I didn't hear you. Are you okay?" James's concern didn't even register in my consciousness. I looked up at him, my brown eyes full of malice.

"Not John," I said seconds before I swiped at him. Four ribbons of blood blossomed across his face, surprising us both. It fueled my anger. I screamed as I slashed him to pieces, my body covered in his blood and gore as he took his last breath. I whispered one last thing to him as he died, an accusation, a curse. "Not John."

It was all I could say, my mantra as I killed the impostor, the betrayer. My chest heaved with exertion. I turned toward Tommy who looked at me with respect and adoration in his eyes. Now that my rage had dimmed, he easily dodged my flimsy attacks on him, throwing me to the floor and pinning my hands above my head, kissing me harshly.

"You are so unbelievably beautiful. Let's go." He helped me to my feet and walked me to the door. He walked down the hall and waited for me at another door. Blood dripped down my broken body as I walked over the pristine carpet. I didn't care. That stupid flicker of hope was a beacon, calling me towards the door. Inside was another bedroom.

It reeked of sagebrush in the fall. I could've wept at the smell. The scent of herbs and blood wafted out to me, and I knew I was finally seeing John. I leaned heavily on the doorframe, knowing I didn't have the energy to take another step, but needing to see him for myself. He was my person, my responsibility, and I had to know he was healing.

"Natasha? Dear gods, what have they done to you?" he whispered, eyes round in his gaunt face. He tried to get up and come toward me but winced with the pain of movement. A woman stood next to his bed, clucking over him. I knew I didn't have much time to talk. Nicholas wouldn't want us conspiring against him. What we could do in our weakened state, I had no idea, but I knew Nicholas wouldn't risk his life on that.

"Real John. Killed not John. Run. Be safe. Leave me." My voice was a strangled whisper of sound, but I had to tell him. I hoped he could hear and understand me. Tears came to his eyes as he nodded slightly. Tommy scooped me into his arms and carried me back to the tank.

The flames licked across my body as I lay, unmoving, where they left me. This was the eighth time they'd danced on my skin, and I no longer cried out or struggled against them. I wanted them to finish their job, to end this suffering. I was tired of the pain.

It seemed as if I'd felt nothing but pain since I mated. It was supposed to be a joyous time, a time when I was finally whole. Instead, all I felt was anger, hurt, and pain. Raif had discarded me, possibly lied to me. My sister had betrayed me with her secrets. James betrayed his brother and me to a psychopath. Stephan abandoned me when I needed him the most, and now this physical pain matched my internal suffering. I just wanted it all to end. I didn't want to live this life anymore.

The flames shifted. Rain pattered down on my blistered skin. This was different. I heard the crackle of lightning, the roar of the thunder past the sounds of the dying flames. I sighed, wondering what new torture I was to endure, surprised that I even cared. I wished they'd just let me die.

The flames disappeared with the storm. The winds picked up, and all around me, I could hear screams of death. They were different from my screams. Mine held agony, the knowledge that I'd live through the pain. Theirs held finality, knowledge that this would be the last sound their bodies uttered. I shuddered and prayed that the angel of death would have mercy and take me next.

The gentle rain never picked up around me, and the winds never touched me. It was as if I were the vortex of the storm, the eye of the hurricane. All around me was death and destruction, but I would remain untouched. I cursed my luck. I prayed for death, and it refused to answer my call. I didn't have the energy to move, let alone mastermind an escape. I could only lie on the stone surface and pray the pain would go away.

I heard voices through the storm. In my delirium, I envisioned them as the angels of death, come to decide how I was to die. The small ember of hope flared as I thought I heard Stephan and John looking for me. It couldn't be them. Tommy told me I'd killed John, thinking he was someone else, and Stephan abandoned me long ago. I was delusional, my pain-addled mind playing tricks on me to give me hope. I imagined them talking about me.

"She should be in the center of the storm. Look for the rain," Stephan's voice yelled against the wind.

"There! I see her, at least, I think it's her." John's excited voice echoed in the wind. "Oh, dear gods! What have they done to her?" His horror filled exclamation was quickly followed by sounds of retching.

"Oh, Tasha, forgive me for being so late. John, hand me the wrap. We need to get her home immediately." Stephan's voice was filled with regret.

The rain stopped, and I felt a soft fabric settle on my skin. It felt like silk. It was the first thing to touch my body that didn't cause pain. I moaned. Strong arms lifted me in a gentle embrace. Stephan's ozone scent enveloped me, and I passed out.

I came to in a bed. I was damp, the taste of blood was in my mouth, and strong arms were curled protectively around me. My skin didn't hurt any longer, but it was still faintly pink. I rubbed my hands on my smooth arms and marveled at my body's healing capabilities. I was still completely hairless, but my skin was growing back without a mark on it.

The body behind me stiffened for a second before relaxing and gently releasing me from its embrace. Stephan's weight shifted as he sat up.

"Where are you going?" I croaked out, voice husky and sore from being abused. I didn't want Stephan to leave. I was afraid he'd leave, and I'd wake up and be back in the caverns.

"I'm just getting you another wet sheet and some blood. I'll return shortly." He wouldn't look at me. He kept his feelings completely hidden from me.

I sat up, testing my newly healed skin on the satin sheets. I didn't hurt. For the first time since I was taken, I felt okay. The sheets were damp, but not uncomfortable. They molded to my skin and were soothing to the touch. Hesitantly, I reached up to my face.

My skin was intact, and I had eyebrows and eyelashes. I could have wept with joy. My shaking hands went to my burned scalp.

I was afraid I'd be bald, that my hair would never grow back from the repeated singeing it took. I liked my hair. I really didn't want to lose it. My fingers ran through slight stubble across my scalp. It was soft, baby fine, and mine. Stephan walked in as I was petting myself. I blushed and brought my hands back to the covers. I pulled them up high and he sighed.

"I've already seen you, Tasha. We have to change the coverings every couple of hours to make certain you have fresh water for healing. This was the only way we could keep you wet. You screamed and thrashed against everything else. I promise not to ravish you." He kept his eyes averted from me as he held out another water-soaked satin sheet. He came closer and quickly removed my damp sheet to replace it with the one he held in his arms. I noticed he was soaked as well. He must have stayed with me the whole time, wrapped up in the water. I smiled at that knowledge.

"Here, drink this. It'll help you heal faster. I have John working on breakfast for you. I'm not sure when you ate last, but you need sustenance other than my blood." He held out a cup filled with dark liquid. I reached out for it. As soon as it was in my hand, he bolted to the door. "Forgive me for failing you, my lady." He finally met my eyes. His were filled with unshed tears. Remorse coated his whispered words. My heart broke.

"You didn't fail me. You saved me." It still hurt to talk. I drank his still-warm blood and felt content for the first time in a long time. I whispered one last thing, not really caring if he heard the need in my voice. "Please, don't leave me."

He moved to the side of the bed. I patted the spot next to me. It was all I could do. I didn't want him to leave, but it hurt to speak. He crawled onto the bed next to me, cautious not to jostle my body. My lips curved with relief. He collapsed in my arms. His body shook with his sobs as he clutched my waist. Even as he clung, weeping in my lap, he was careful of my healing tissue.

"Forgive me. Thank Poseidon we found you, but please forgive me! I am so grateful that you still live! Thank the gods." He mumbled into my belly as I stroked his hair. He whispered nonsense in his native tongue. His tears mixed with the water already soaking my skin, and I held him until they subsided.

"Stephan, I'm tired. Lay with me?" I whispered as his weeping slowed. He blinked up at me, his tearstained face in awe.

"I would do anything for you." He blinked at me and for the first time, let me see the love he held for me. He would never act upon it, but I knew then that the kiss we shared in our dream was somehow real. It had been something he'd wanted, something we both wanted.

He cocooned me in the soaking sheet, draping a corner across my head, and curled up behind me. His arms wrapped protectively around me just as they had been when I woke a few minutes earlier. I drifted off into a peaceful, healing sleep.

When I woke, hours later, I was starving and alone. I sat up abruptly, wondering where Stephan was. The room was dark with the night, but the covers kept me centered in reality. I wasn't in the cavern. I was at Stephan's. I was safe.

I got out of bed and stood for the first time since seeing John healing in bed. My legs were shaky but held. I walked to the bathroom to use the facilities and take a shower. The water was heavenly. My hair had grown another inch while I slept and was just starting to take on some curl. The little hairs on my arms were back, as were the hairs on my legs. I couldn't bring myself to shave off those happy little nubs; I was too excited to be getting back to normal.

I dried myself off gently and turned to look in the mirror. I was spotted red and pink. Every inch of my body had burned and been abraded by dirt and wind. I had a gash high on my hip that I didn't remember getting. It was healing but looked as if it'd leave a scar. It was the only mark on my body. My eyes were the same since I'd changed—dark brown flecked with teal. The only thing different was my hair. It was completely black. The red and brown highlights I'd had since changing had disappeared. Maybe they'd come back after some time in the sun. It was also baby fine. I hoped it would go back to normal.

Satisfied that externally, I was fine, I left the bathroom in search of clothing. Stephan entered the bedroom just as I did. He stared at me, mouth dropping in shock. He averted his gaze just seconds after I saw the lust. I walked to the bed and grabbed the damp cover.

"Where are my clothes? I'm feeling better now and would like to get dressed." My voice was stronger. It didn't hurt so much to talk anymore.

"They're down the hall in your room. I can take you there if you'd like." He glanced back up at me with a tentative smile on his lips.

"That'd be nice," I said and took his hand in mine. I smiled up at him. "After that, I want to eat. I'm starving."

He laughed as my stomach growled, accenting my statement. It was nice to hear him laugh. I was worried that he'd continue to be standoffish and our fragile relationship would continue to be strained. He walked me to my room and waited while I changed.

I dressed in loose clothing and followed him back to his room where John was waiting with breakfast. The smells of hot chocolate, muffins, and ham couldn't distract me from the sight of his completely healed and whole body. I ran to him, hugging him close, needing to feel his body to make certain it wasn't my delusional mind playing tricks on me.

"You're okay. It wasn't a dream. You really are okay!" I smiled at him, patting his arms, chest, and face to verify that he really was whole and alive. I couldn't believe how good he looked.

"Thanks to you," he said, eyes filling with tears as he hugged me back. "You really shouldn't have done that. But I thank you from the bottom of my heart. Now eat."

He sat with us, and they both watched as I scarfed the food down, moaning in contentment. I'd eaten enough to fill two grown men before I realized they were still staring in fascination. I blushed.

"What? I haven't eaten in...well I don't know how long. How long have I been here? How long was I in that house?" I shuddered as a sudden chill ran up my spine.

"Tomorrow is the night of the Hunter's Moon. It's been two weeks since you were taken." Stephan's quiet voice was filled with regret. My fork fell from my fingers.

"Well then." I cleared my throat, trying not to sound horrified. "It's been two weeks since I've eaten. Do either of you know what happened? How did they know I'd be at my house alone?" I choked out the words, trying to sound more together than I felt. Two weeks. It felt like an eternity. I returned to eating even though the food now felt like lead in my stomach.

"It was James. He betrayed us to Nicholas in hopes of getting revenge on you for humiliating him. He drugged me. My own brother kidnapped and helped them torture me." He didn't even try to hide the pain in his voice. "I'm so sorry, Natasha. I never thought he'd be capable of doing something like that. At least we don't have to worry about him anymore." A tear slid silently down John's face. He ignored it.

"Oh my God. That really happened?" I looked at them in horror, food forgotten with the realization that the murder of the one I called Not John truly took place. It wasn't just a dream inflicted by my pain-addled mind. My stomach churned as I thought of the other memories I'd thought were dreams. I prayed they weren't real, but knew my prayers fell on deaf ears. Forcing myself away from these thoughts, I said the only thing I could. "I'm so sorry, John." He nodded. His sad smile telling me he understood but was still grieving for the brother who betrayed us.

"Are they all dead, then?" I whispered.

"Yes," Stephan said, his voice firm and clipped. He didn't want to talk about it and neither did I. Not yet. The wounds were still too fresh. There was one thing I had to know though. I couldn't wait another minute, or I'd chicken out and force myself to believe it was all part of the horrific nightmare I was placing all my memories into. Closing my eyes to say a quick prayer that I was wrong, I turned and looked directly at Stephan.

"Nicholas told me some things about the prophecy and my mating I didn't want to believe. I have to know. I deserve to know." My voice shook as I asked what I didn't want to believe. "Nicholas said Raif has to die, that he knew of his death from the beginning.

Is it true?" I had to hear it from Stephan. He couldn't meet my eyes, shattering my heart. "Why didn't you tell me?" I whispered, throat tight with the pain of betrayal.

"I wanted you to be able to survive on your own before I told you. I wasn't certain how you'd react." His voice was soft, regret thick in the air. "Raifuku should have told you before you agreed to mate. My heart truly grieves for you." He slumped in his chair, head hanging in remorse. I still couldn't believe it. They had to be wrong. Raif couldn't die.

"He knew I'd never agree to the mating, had I known. Is there any way to stop him?" I knew the answer before I asked, but still, I hoped. He looked up at me, tears pooling in his silver orbs. Gently, he shook his head. "Is that it then? Is there anything else I should know? Anything else that's been kept from me?" My voice was cold, bitter with pain.

"There's still much you need to know about who you are and what you're capable of. However, in regard to the prophecy, that will be completed when a full-blooded Atlantean mates and allows his blood to coat Poseidon's alter. Only then will we be free of the curse that has hidden us from civilization for the past eleven thousand years."

"Could Nicholas have prevented it?" I shuddered at the memory of what was done to me. Stephan vibrated in anger.

"No. He would've eventually killed you. That may have prevented the fulfillment, or it would've succeeded in completing the prophecy. We're uncertain if a mixed blood's death would be sufficient. No one's been able to give Cleito her tears back before. Nicholas wouldn't have risked killing you if he truly wished to remove the threat of fulfillment." Anger gave way to a deep pain as he spoke. "Once mated, the only true way to remove the bond is the death of a mate. The survivor, however, usually joins their mate shortly after death." He wasn't talking to me anymore. He was lost in his own thoughts, his own pain that he kept hidden from the world. I went pale at his words.

"So, I might die when Raif does." My voice was monotone. Maybe that was for the best.

"The bonds of mating are soul deep. You and Raifuku are truly two bodies sharing one soul. Normally, mates live the remainder of their long mortal lives together, strengthening the bonds until they're so thick the mortal bodies literally cannot live without each other. There's only one that I know of that has survived the death of their mate, and he almost went mad." He shook his head. "You and Raifuku haven't been mated long. Your bonds, while permanent and unbreakable, are still weak. You have an abnormal mating, one that should allow you to survive Raifuku's death."

"I can't deal with this right now. I can't process this in front of you." I'd seen the love Stephan had for me reflected in his eyes. How was I supposed to grieve for my soul mate in front of him? "Is there any place I can go, alone? Or at least somewhat alone?" I knew better than to just run off. Nicholas cured me of any desire I had to be completely alone.

"I will take you someplace that's safe for you." Stephan held the door open for me and led me to his car. I was shaking with anger, hurt, and fear. How could they have kept this from me? How could Raif have mated with me without telling me it meant his death, and possibly my own? I wished I'd never gone on that stupid cruise. I never would've gone diving and never would've met Raif. My heart clenched.

14

Stephan drove to a secluded rocky area of beach and pointed to a large, flat boulder in the water, about fifty feet from shore.

"I often come here when I need to be alone. I'll wait here for you. Take all the time you need." He turned the radio on low to a jazz station he liked, giving me the illusion of privacy. I got out of the car and walked to the water. It was dark; the almost-full Hunter's Moon cast an eerie blushed glow on the waters. I knew Stephan would be at my side in seconds if I shouted, and I took comfort in that as I dove into the black waters.

I swam out to the boulder, ignoring the light stings of the jellyfish as I went. They were but an irritant after my time with Nicholas. The rock was slick, smooth from the continued beatings of the waves, and thick with algae growing all around, making it difficult to obtain purchase as I climbed up. I made it, slicing my palm on a jagged edge as I did so.

I crawled to the middle of the boulder and sat. I wanted to cry, needed to, but was completely unable to do so. Instead, I watched as the blood dripped from my palm into the salty ocean waters. I watched as it dripped until the wound sealed shut, proof that I was still different, that I would never be human again.

Everything compounded with the sealing of that small cut, coming together in a finality that rocked me to my core. I now fully understood what Stephan meant when he said I'd given up so much.

I'd lost my family, my old, ignorant life, and my humanity. Now I was going to lose my mate and probably my life. For what? A civilization that had existed just fine in the depths of the ocean for millennia, cursed by fate for overstepping their place in life? It wasn't fair. They didn't even want to change. They liked the way things were. Not only had I lost everything, but the people I was trying to help kept trying to kill me.

I screamed my frustrations into the air. I screamed until my throat was sore. I cursed a god I wasn't sure I believed in for allowing me to go through this. I cursed Poseidon for being an ass and allowing his people to be such fools. Finally, I cursed Raif. I hated him in that moment. But only for a moment. As I cursed and yelled at him through the winds and eight miles of ocean, I collapsed in wracking, tearless sobs.

I understood why he hadn't told me everything. In his own way, he was trying to protect me as he righted the wrongs that were done to his people. He'd known what mating meant for him from the beginning, yet he'd still done it. My heart broke, knowing I couldn't even say goodbye. The waves crashed against the boulder, misting me with the salty water. The ocean's waves allowed me to feel the wetness on my cheeks for the first time since mating, giving me the illusion of tears.

Strong arms gathered me up, holding me protectively against a chest I was becoming way too familiar with. Stephan's unique scent enveloped me as he rocked me gently in his arms, whispering in a language I didn't understand.

"I can't even say goodbye," I whispered as I sobbed tearlessly onto his shoulder. "Everything's been taken from me, even my goodbye."

He held me long into the night, rocking me gently as the waves crashed all around us. He continued to hold me long after my sniffles subsided, and I let him. I needed the comfort. Truth was, there was only one other pair of arms I'd rather have around me but couldn't. Sitting on a boulder in the Atlantic Ocean, I finally allowed myself to admit that my feelings for Stephan went so much deeper than friendship. If not for my bond to Raif, I'd think I was in love with Stephan.

I looked up at him then. He watched the waves as silent tears streamed down his face. He was lost in another place, another time, but his pain was as fresh as mine. I wrapped my arms around him, returning the comfort he gave me.

We sat there, each living our own version of hell on that rock, waves splashing about, completely oblivious to our tormented souls. I started to shiver in the early morning light, the spray from the waves cooling me to my core. His arms tightened around me, warming more than just my skin. I snuggled closer, my face buried in his warmth.

"Do you want to talk about it?" I asked in a voice that was scratchy and hoarse from crying. His smile was weak.

"Her name was Olivia." It was all he said for a very long time. I was used to his pauses by now and waited for him to decide if he wanted to explain or not. It was his story to tell, or keep if he so desired, even if it was one I hoped he'd share. "She was a merchant's daughter. I was trading, using that as an excuse to look for new donors, when I saw her. She was small, like you, with lavender eyes. It was the eyes that did it. She could've been a wrinkled old crone with three teeth for all I cared. As soon as our eyes met, I knew." His voice was soft, and he clung to me, anchoring him to this time as his mind wandered into the past.

"I stole her away that very night. I told her all about our race, about *alma xemelgas*, what she'd be risking if she went through with mating with me. She told me she'd been waiting for me her entire life, and even a moment in my arms would be worth anything." Tears resumed falling silently down his face, and he had to clear his throat before continuing. "We were mated in private by the end of the week. I knew there were factions of Atlanteans that didn't want the prophecy to be fulfilled. They would go to any lengths to prevent it, and I wouldn't risk ending her life, or mine, for that of my people. We lived hidden from the world for her protection. It was heaven.

"I knew there were people, like Nicholas, who would hurt her simply for knowing me."

"Why?" I asked.

"Power," he whispered. "I was the High Priest, the highest title we had when we sank. That's why I became the leader on the surface. If those that opposed me were able to get to Olivia, they could control me. I'd do anything for my mate. Anyone would."

I thought of Raif and pain lanced through my heart. By mating with me, and sending me back to the surface, he was looking out for his people, not for me. He looked out for his people, even though it cost him his mate and his life. I couldn't help but be angry with him at that knowledge. Stephan continued.

"Olivia knew the risks when we mated. She knew what Poseidon would try to have us do if he found out about her. Still, she eagerly became my mate. She was everything to me." He sighed deeply, shuddering at the memories as he gathered his thoughts. "We had a son.

"He was three when we were discovered. I was headed home from the club when I felt her terror. She was strong; I'd trained her well. Even with her training and the instinct to protect her young, she was overtaken. I arrived at the house in time to watch as they were split open, their blood soaking the ground." Only his silent tears betrayed the pain he still felt from that memory.

"They thought only of preventing the prophecy. Had they asked, they would've known I'd never willingly separate from Olivia just to see my homeland again. She was worth more to me than that. I'd give anything to be with her again.

"They thought I'd die then, with my family. I didn't. I saw her blood splattering the lawn, seeping from her delicate throat, and went mad. In a rage, I slaughtered them all. Ten were sent to murder my wife and child; none lived past the night. I tortured information out of the one that spilled her blood. I enjoyed watching him suffer. He told me who sent them and why. He would've told me anything I wanted to hear by the end, just to stop the pain. I didn't care. I knew there'd never be a release from my pain, so why should I grant him leniency?

"Eventually, even my torture was taken from me. The coward died. The pain of losing Olivia and Caleb became too much for me to bear, and I passed out. When I came to, more than a week had passed. I was left lying in a field of decomposing corpses. I knew I had to dispose of the bodies and give my *amada* a proper burial, but I couldn't. I had to eliminate the cause of her demise, the man who orchestrated the whole thing, Mneseus."

I gasped, horrified that Raif's father could be so heartless and cruel as to murder an innocent woman and child. No wonder Stephan hated Raif so much. I opened my lips to say something, and Stephan stopped me with a slight shake of his head.

"No, *miña mascota,* I've never spoken of this to anyone before; I fear if you interrupt, I'll never finish. During my week of unconsciousness, something happened to me. I became more than I was before. I was different, yet completely the same. It's difficult to explain, but I felt more complete than even after I'd mated. My soul was complete, but my heart was empty. It was a terrible feeling.

"Forcing myself to do what was right, I piled the bodies of the murderers and burned them to ash. I took the remains of my wife and son to the ocean. There, I gave them a funeral fit for kings. I placed them together on a small raft with a sail. Controlling the winds, I watched as they were gently taken out to sea. When they were far enough away, I called upon the element of fire to set them aflame. It was a heartbreakingly beautiful sight.

"Until you came, our house had remained barren. I never wanted to see it again. I didn't know even if I could. It was no longer a peaceful haven. It had become a place of death. You've given it life again, after so many centuries of neglect. I thank you for that." He gave me a shy smile, erasing some of his haunted expression.

"What I did next still haunts my dreams. I didn't set out only to kill Mneseus; I decimated his entire clan. You and Raifuku are quite possibly the only true Changers left of his line. There are a few vampires he created that remain, but even they are reaching the close of their long existence. The oldest of his creations is four-hundred-twenty-two years of age. She will live another six hundred years before the madness of the centuries weighs her down and I'm forced to end her existence. I loathe that day.

"Mneseus knew I was coming for him. Even without the brutal murders of his clan, he knew I'd be after him. Truth be told, I should have destroyed him decades before, but I couldn't bear to have any more Atlantean blood on my hands. I was tired of being the executioner of our people. Mneseus and I were the oldest survivors, and the years weighed heavily on us. Olivia saved me from the madness, and I'd hoped that Mneseus would've found the same salvation.

"He was hiding in his South American compound when I found him. It was like a castle, but more heavily fortified. I blew the doors off, smashing the stone walls with hurricane force winds of fire that succeeded in obliterating half of my opposition.

"Mneseus sat in a square garden in the middle of the compound on a king's chair. I reigned in my temper, holding my need for vengeance back by a thread. I wanted to know why he had her killed. Truthfully, I wanted to rip his head off with my bare hands. Being destroyed by my power was too good for a man such as him. As I approached his makeshift throne, I demanded an explanation. His response rocked me to my core.

"'You've been neglecting your responsibilities as Poseidon's High Priest.' That's what he told me. He said that since I'd mated, I'd been too distracted looking out for Olivia's safety to pay attention to the threats to my own race. That was why he'd killed her. Because she was a *distraction* to me." He said the word "distraction" like it was poison he was spitting from his mouth. "He said her loss was a worthy sacrifice for the good of our people. I saw through all his excuses. He wanted to die. He needed to provoke my anger so that I would kill him. In the end, the great Master of Arms was nothing but a weak, bitter old man." Stephan kept his eyes on the horizon as he spoke, lost in the memory. "Even so, he couldn't go without a fight.

"He leapt into the air, changing into an abomination in the blink of an eye. He had the legs of a bear, head of a wolf, tail of a scorpion; his chest was protected by a thick shell of a creature I didn't even know, and he had the paws of a lion. He was the chimera I'd heard about that was terrorizing these lands. I gaped in horror as he stood in front of me.

"He charged and without thought, I blasted him with a bolt of lightning. It was a move that surprised us both, as it wasn't a power held by those of Poseidon's lineage. Before he could regain his bearings, I called upon my connections to the water element. Using all the power I held, I called forth every droplet of water from his body until he was nothing more than a dry husk before me. I took his head in my hands, twisted, and yanked it off. His body thumped to the floor, converting once again to the figure of the man I'd grown up with. I burned his head and body, letting his ashes float away on the breeze, just as I had the rest of his clan. I then went in search of what he'd hidden away for so long, knowing it wouldn't be good.

"In the depths of his castle, I found them. Dozens of creations chained and tortured. Some were already dead from his ministrations; others begged for death. I walked through the dungeons, each horror imprinting itself on my mind. The knowledge that he'd been right, that I'd ignored the rumors in hopes someone else would take my place, smacked into me with every abomination I came across. I'd allowed this to happen by ignoring and denying my position. Vowing to never allow this again, I opened the last door.

"I won't betray Victoria's trust by revealing what I saw. Just know it was worse than anything I'd ever seen, until I saw you in Nicholas's chamber." He shuddered. "When I walked into the room, she stared at me with her blue eyes blazing in defiance. I freed all I could and destroyed the rest. The ones that were freed were sent to live with leaders who would properly train and care for them. Victoria stayed with me of her own volition. She didn't trust anyone else. Without her, I was lost with the fulfillment of my revenge. She gave me a purpose, a reason to go on. She's also my constant reminder of what would happen if I neglected my responsibilities to my people again.

"It's been 317 years and forty-five days since Olivia died. I miss her each day but am now more complete without her. I'm a being that was designed by the Creator, one who is whole and complete in every way. It's a strange and glorious feeling; one that I treasure." He finally looked at me, tears drying in streaks down his face and pooling in his eyes. I felt his pain and determination almost as clearly as I could feel Raif's emotions.

"I will not allow you to die. When it's time for your mate to complete the prophecy, you will stay with me, and I will force you to go on, if I must. You will not perish for our people." He was firm with his resolve.

"How will you know?" There was no way to communicate with a sunken island.

"Atreyu and I are able to talk, like you and I did when you were with Nicholas. We are both strong Dream-Walkers and have communicated for centuries. Not only that, but together we can open a portal into Poseidon's temple. It's difficult and drains us both for days, but it's how I get my blood supply."

"Wait a minute. You mean I could see Raif again? I could say goodbye when it's time?" Hope surged through my veins. He nodded.

"If you would like to say goodbye, I've already arranged it with Atreyu. The ceremony's planned for midnight tomorrow."

15

I couldn't believe I was going to see Raif again. I paced my bedroom, thinking of all the things that needed to be said between us. I was a bundle of nerves at the thought of being able to be with him again. Stephan explained that he hadn't been convinced I'd want to say goodbye, that I'd want to watch Raif die. Raif was my mate, the other half of my soul. If I couldn't figure out a way to free him from his destiny, I at least wanted to hold him as he left this world.

"Take the time to sleep," Stephan admonished. "You need to heal, and the best way to do that is through sleep."

"How could I possibly sleep?" I snapped at him. My stomach was in knots at the thought of what was about to happen. I couldn't admit to Stephan that a part of me was still hoping beyond hope that there would be some way to stop this. My heart broke at the thought of seeing Raif again just to let him slip away.

"Here, drink this. It has a potion that will allow you to drift off." At my skeptical look, he continued. "I vow to wake you with plenty of time to see your mate. Sleep, Tasha. Please."

It was the please. Pleases always did me in. I took the tea, pacing and worrying as I absentmindedly sipped it. There had to be a way to prevent this. I wasn't ready to lose Raif and possibly lose myself in the process. There had to be a loophole. If only I had more time. I'd be able to research and find a way out of this mess. If I only...if I could just...

The thoughts were blurring together in my mind. I couldn't follow the thread of a single one. My body was heavy and disoriented. I looked at the empty cup in my hands. *Dang, that worked fast!*

The cup rolled out of my numb fingers and onto the floor as my body fell against the side of the mattress. My head flopped back against the middle of the bed. As soon as my head hit the soft comforter, I was out, still trying to figure out if I was grateful or angry that I'd let Stephan drug me.

Hours later, I finally met the elusive Marcy. She was a petite girl with a heart shaped face, huge blue eyes, and a shapely body. Everything about her was tiny, except her eyes. They were filled with laughter as she woke me up.

"It's about time you started coming around. If you sleep any longer, you'll miss the whole ceremony. We can't have that now, can we?" She smiled her thin lips as she bounced over to the bathroom. I heard the shower start and groaned.

Whatever Stephan had put in my tea left one hell of a hangover. I sat up on the edge of my bed with my head in my hands.

Sighing with resignation, I ran my fingers through my hair to remove the lingering feeling of fatigue from my psyche. I stopped abruptly, the length of my hair finally registering in my sleep-addled brain. It was back! I gathered the soft strands in my fists, smiling at the slight pull against my scalp. This was one myth I could get on board with.

I remembered a movie from when I was a teen, where a child vampire cut her hair only to scream as it immediately grew back. Mine wasn't as instantaneous, but it was interesting that it grew so fast. I wondered, for a moment, if it would always do that. Checking the rest of me, I was surprised to see that my skin was no longer splotchy either. I still had a faint pinkish hue, but for the most part, I was me again. I had a dopey grin on my face, both hands fisted in my hair as Marcy walked back into the bedroom. She laughed with me, not understanding why I was laughing, but glad to share cheer with someone.

I ran past her to look in the bathroom mirror. I stripped off my clothes and stood in front of the mirror. Even the cut on my hip was disappearing. Outside, I was whole, normal, and complete. I could sense the internal damage but knew time would be the only healer for those wounds. Stephan wouldn't have a magic sleeping potion to fix that. With the sight of my hair and almost healed body, I had hope.

I smiled at my reflection, pleased that Raif's last image of me wouldn't be that of a half-healed woman, but the woman he remembered. My smile fell as my thoughts brought me back to what was going to happen in a few short hours. That thought sobered me as I bathed.

Marcy brought a handful of sweet-smelling scrubs for me, along with some ridiculous oils and creams. I picked one that reminded me of my time in Atlantis. It was a sweet, tangy scent with just a hint of mint. It was crisp, clean, and made me feel sexy.

She was there when I stepped out of the shower, towel in hand. Within minutes, the petite woman had me dried, my hair styled, and was working on my nails. I halfheartedly protested the attention, but Marcy waved her hands to dismiss me and was done before I knew it. I was still trying to figure out how this small woman managed to dominate the room when she started applying makeup on me.

"Wait, Marcy. Not that I don't appreciate what you're doing, but I don't usually wear makeup." I smiled at her as I leaned away from a brush. She smiled back.

"You don't really need it anyway. Let's get you dressed." Her eyes glittered in excitement. She brought out every protective and caring instinct I had in my bones. Bouncing out of the bathroom, she hummed with energy and excitement. "Stephan should be ready to start soon. You're so lucky to do this with him!"

A minute later, I strolled back into the bedroom. Marcy had already picked out a beautiful dress and matching shoes. It was strapless with a sweetheart neckline and flowed to the floor. The top was a deep teal that faded into the deep black of the nighttime ocean waters as it reached the floor.

Marcy zipped around me, and before I knew it, I was draped in the beautiful dress. She smiled, adjusting my pendant to sit at my cleavage. It fit perfectly.

"It's beautiful," I whispered. I swayed side to side, watching as the skirt billowed in waves around my ankles. I felt like a princess. "Thank you."

"This was all Stephan. He knew you'd want to look nice tonight, but I don't think he expected this. You look absolutely stunning. We should get going." Her excitement was infectious. I couldn't help but smile back at her. I understood now why John liked being with her so much.

She led me down the stairs, continuing on to the underbelly of the club and into a place I'd yet to explore. At the end of the staircase was a large, heavy door. She motioned me toward it.

"This is as far as I go. Good luck tonight." She smiled again, running back up the stairs behind me. I listened as she bounded up the stairs and into the club beyond. My nerves returned as the hidden door to the club closed behind her. I wasn't sure what to expect tonight and wasn't sure I could just stand by and watch as Raif was killed.

Squaring my shoulders, I opened the door and walked into the room from my dream. The door slid to a quiet close as I took in my surroundings. A thousand candles were lit, with incense burning on the altar in the center. Standing with his back to me, Stephan lit more incense.

He was surrounded by candles. The entire room seemed to flicker. I stood in the entryway, unsure of myself. I could feel a hum of power building and knew Stephan had already started. I cleared my throat.

He paused and glanced over his bare shoulder. Whatever he was about to say died on his lips. His magnesium eyes heated, echoing with the feelings I hid in my heart. I hoped my own feelings were hidden better than his.

I wasn't sure how someone could love two completely different men so deeply, but as I stood there, looking at Stephan, knowing I was about to see Raif, I felt twin pangs of love and betrayal. Raif held my soul, my very essence, but I could no longer deny that Stephan held my heart. I didn't know when it had happened exactly, but I knew in the very fibers of my being that it was true. I loved them both, deeply, passionately, and without reservation.

"Thank you for the dress. It's beautiful." I smiled shyly at him. "Where do you want me?" He blushed, eyes darkening at my question. It took me a moment to understand his expression and grasp the undertones of what I'd asked. I returned his blush. "I-I mean...what I meant was..." I stuttered over the words until he rescued me.

"Step carefully over the candles and stand here with me." He watched as I lifted my skirts to my knees, revealing my bare feet as I gently stepped over the candles. I stood next to him at the altar, the incense swirling around us with thick, cloying smoke. It instantly relaxed my tense muscles, and I inhaled more of the tangy scent.

"You are so beautiful," Stephan whispered. I tensed slightly at his words, memories of another voice stating that very same thing flashed in my head. He looked startled at my reaction.

"I'm sorry," I whispered, knowing he wasn't Tommy. Tommy was dead, and I was safe. I could smell Stephan's distinct scent under the smell of incense and knew he'd never cause me pain like that. My face flushed with shame, and I ducked my head so he wouldn't see the pain that must be evident on my face. I still couldn't talk about my time at Nicholas's house. "Thank you. Do I need to do anything?"

He took a step closer to me so our bodies were a breath apart. Gently, he cupped my face in his hands, leaving goose bumps on my flesh. He lifted my chin with his hands so I could see the truth in his eyes.

"You are perfection." He whispered the words, and I trembled. He blinked, ending the spell and returning to the task at hand. "I need your left hand. This spell requires the blood of the one who will pass into the portal. It takes your essence and blends it with Atreyu's, connecting this room with the one in Atlantis. You may feel some odd sensations, a pulling against your aura, but stay by my side until I tell you otherwise."

I gave him a trembling hand. I couldn't tell if it was fear or desire causing my body to shiver. I was going to see my mate. Stephan held my hand and sliced the meaty part of my palm, just under my thumb. Blood welled and dripped steadily into a cup he held underneath. It didn't take long for the cup to fill, and the wound closed within moments, leaving a small smear of blood on my palm. He brought it to his lips, licking it gently with his tongue. Taking the cup, he poured a thin circle around us, in front of the burning circle of candles. He spoke words I didn't understand under his breath as he walked the circle. When he reached the beginning of the circle of blood, it closed with an audible *pop*. I could feel the power vibrating within the confines of the circle. My body hummed with energy.

Stephan drew a line with chalk on the floor, coating it immediately with my blood. He continued his chant, the power building as he spoke. From the line of chalk, a dark swirling doorway grew. I watched in fascination as it pulled itself out of the floor, the dark mist beckoning me closer. I'd taken a small step closer to the portal before realizing I'd even moved.

Blinking, I shook my head to clear it from the portal's call. I had to wait for Stephan. His back was to me, sweat pouring off his body in little rivers. He was shaking with the effort it took to call forth the portal between the two lands.

"It's time." His voice was husky and heavily accented. His eyes swirled with power as he gestured toward the portal. I walked in before my nerves could convince me otherwise.

16

The portal opened into the most lavish room I'd ever seen. The walls were made from the ruby-colored orichalcum, polished to a shine. Pieces hung from the ceiling, cut to reflect the sun's rays into a beautiful, glimmering, blood-red hue around the room. Fantastic murals of the sea were painted on the walls. The one I was looking at was centered on the wall over the room's only doorway. It was the sea at twilight—calm, peaceful, and inviting. The stars were just starting to twinkle in the heavens. It was breathtakingly realistic.

Underneath another elaborately painted mural of the sea at sunrise was an altar. The water was shimmering with anticipation at what the dawn would bring, and the colors of the rainbow-hued sky glistened on the waves. The orichalcum altar was on a raised dais, also carved of orichalcum. Scenes of Poseidon using his trident to control the waters in defense of his lands coated the front of the altar. Images of boats capsizing, bodies being consumed by the sea, and creatures lurking beneath the waves were carved in vivid detail. Lying motionless on the glossy slab was Raif.

My heart stuttered in my chest. Raif. After all this time, there he was. I ran toward him, my steps echoing oddly in this room. I knew now that I was in Poseidon's temple. I slowed as I reached the steps that led up to the altar, my heart fluttering in my chest in anticipation and fear. I could feel the echo of Raif like a second beat in my chest. The intensity of his life force was overwhelming. I knew he wasn't dead or dying. Why wasn't he moving? Surely, he'd heard my steps and could feel my presence, as I could feel his.

"Raif?" I said hesitantly. My voice echoed hollowly in my ears. His fingers twitched at the sound. Before either of us could do anything more, a striking man appeared between the altar and me. He was older than Raif, with long, peppered hair that hung in waves down to his waist. He had broad shoulders, a lean waist, and powerful legs. From the back, I could picture this man as a much older version of Raif.

He turned to look at me. My breath left in a gasp. His eyes swirled with the raging waters of the ocean. They were so captivating; I could barely register the rest of him. He held power. It radiated out of him, knocking me back a step. He looked at me with such anguish, awe, and love my knees went weak.

"Poseidon?" My breathy whisper left in a gasp. It could be no other. He inclined his head, one side of his mouth curving into a secret smile. "Am I too late?" My heart faltered. Poseidon shook his head. My breath left me in an audible sigh of relief. I closed my eyes and thanked whatever deity was listening that I still had a chance to say goodbye. "Why is he lying so still?"

"He asked to be placed in stasis so he could die in his sleep, without pain." I started at the sound of Atreyu's voice. I'd overlooked him standing off to the side, in the shadows. "Poseidon granted him this request, knowing he could do nothing else to ease Raifuku's pain. I'm pleased you came. This is how it should be." Atreyu's voice echoed with fatigue and power. There was so much beauty I was missing, but I couldn't bring myself to look at anything but the man lying motionless on the altar before me.

"I'm not here to stop you. I just want to be with him. He shouldn't be alone, wondering. Will you let me have one last moment to say goodbye?" My voice was a mere whisper, the enormity of what was happening weighed heavily on my shoulders.

A small thread of anger weaved its way through my pain. The fact that I was asking to say goodbye to my husband, my soul mate, was unfathomable. I held onto that anger and met Poseidon's swirling blue orbs with my brown ones filled with determination. "I take it back. I don't want your permission. This is between Raif and me, and I'll be damned if he dies alone. You will let me pass."

My voice was stronger than I felt. I'd never stood up to a deity before. Poseidon saw my resolve etched in every fiber of my being.

If Raif had to die, he wouldn't be alone. He gave an almost imperceptible nod in Atreyu's direction.

"Your sacrifice for our people will not be forgotten." Poseidon's soft words rumbled throughout the temple like thunder before a storm.

I could only nod in assent, hoping that nod meant Raif would be taken out of stasis and I'd get to say goodbye. My stomach had resumed its churning. I was terrified to see Raif, scared he'd toss me aside, scared he wouldn't and I'd have to watch him die. I didn't know what to do now.

On shaking legs, I forced myself up the three steps to Raif. I was finally going to see him, only to say goodbye. Seeing him lying there, so still and perfect, I didn't think I could just stand aside and watch him die.

My hand shook visibly as I reached out to his face. His chiseled features were as soft as I remembered. I brushed his silken hair away from his cheeks, my fingers searching and memorizing every part of it.

His eyes fluttered open, revealing the impossible teal I'd missed so much. I fell on him, clinging to his chest, wiggling against his body. I needed to be as close as possible to him after months of separation. I was grateful he was still alive, even if only for a few more moments. His arms wrapped tightly around me, crushing me against his chest. I could have stayed in his embrace for eternity.

"Natasha, what are you doing here?" he choked out.

"Saying goodbye. You should've told me. I wouldn't have been okay with it, but you should've told me anyway." I leaned slightly back so I could see his face, still cradled in his arms.

"I couldn't figure out how. This must be done. I hope that in time you can understand and forgive me. I love you, *Amada*." He brushed his hand from the top of my head down my back as he talked. His eyes filled with tears. "I'd forgotten how wonderful you are. Seeing you again makes this task impossible."

"Raif, I do understand. I won't stop you, no matter how much I want to, if this is what you want. I wanted to hold you and say goodbye, so you knew you weren't alone and that I love you." My voice cracked with the pain in my heart. I leaned down and kissed his lips. It was a very soft, chaste, undemanding kiss that instantly set me on fire. He crushed me to him, groaning as he deepened the kiss to something that would have led to greater satisfaction had we not been interrupted by Poseidon's polite cough.

"It's time," I whispered, unable to speak louder past the lump in my throat. "Do you want Atreyu to put you under again?" I was suddenly grateful I couldn't cry, that he'd remember me as strong in these last moments.

He shook his head. "No, *Amada*." I want to feel you in my arms till the end." Tears snaked from his eyes and ran into his hair. He would shed tears for us both. I curled into the crook of his arm and caressed his face as Poseidon came closer.

"I love you."

"*Ata o dus eu te amo,*" he whispered. "I will love you for all of eternity." My throat closed even tighter as my body begged to weep and scream its denial.

Poseidon lifted his trident in the air and brought it down to Raif's chest. Other than a tightening of his hand in mine, Raif didn't move a muscle. I knew it hurt. I felt his pain.

"You are so brave." My voice was thick.

Poseidon pulled the trident out of Raif's chest without a sound. Blood started seeping out of the wounds, soaking me and cascading off the alter, taking his life with it. I held him close to me as the blood poured from the wounds. He looked at me with tears in his eyes.

"*Amada*, my only regret is that I didn't have more time with you. I love you." His words were thick and filled with pain. I placed my fingers on his lips.

"Shh, baby, I know. I love you so much. What can I do?" I gently draped my arm across his chest, holding him as tightly as his wounds would allow. I wished I could cry for him; he deserved my tears.

"Talk to me. Hold me. I want to hear your voice." His breath was labored. I knew he didn't have long now.

I knew he could feel my pain, my love for him, as I could feel his for me. My mind was a blank. What do you say to someone as they bleed to death in your arms? I did the only thing I could think of as I held him tightly in my embrace. I told him a story as I used to with Ashlyn.

"Once upon a time, there was a soul. It was happy and content to play in the water's spray, reflecting light into rainbows. It had never known pain or sadness—only joy and contentment. This soul was pure, innocent, and full of love." My voice cracked as I whispered the words. He interrupted me before I could finish.

"Do you really believe that we'll be whole in the Summerlands? That we'll be together again, as two complete beings?" I could barely hear him. His voice was a whisper on the wind.

"Yes," I whispered back. "We were meant to be as the Creator made us. We'll be together again, whole and perfect, but different from what we started out as. We'll know heartbreak like no other soul before us, and because of that, we'll know love more deeply and profoundly than any that have lived before. We'll be more than when we began and be better for it." His eyelids fluttered closed, and he smiled as he went limp in my arms.

"Raif? Raif? No. Not yet. No!" I screamed in agony, sobbing uncontrollably as I clutched him tightly to me, refusing to let him go. I kissed his lips in denial, desperately holding on to hope.

Strong arms lifted my blood-soaked body from the alter, forcing me to release my hold on Raif. I was weak, sobs wracking my body. I cursed the man who held me, cursed his lineage for putting us in this situation. I begged for Raif to wake, pleaded to wake from this nightmare.

Staring at his body, I knew I'd give anything for him to live again. I wept; the lines of his body forever burned into my memory as the one who had murdered my soul carried me away.

17

Poseidon carried me to a fountain in the corner of the room. He walked through it with me cradled in his arms. I vaguely remembered being placed into Stephan's outstretched arms and hearing Poseidon's rumbling voice telling him to protect me.

Stephan clutched me close to him, and I sobbed even harder. He carried me to his room and placed me on the bed, curling around my body. I don't know how long I wept. It felt like days but was probably only minutes. It was by far the worst day of my life. But not, I'd come to find out, the most painful.

There are three occasions in my short life that I would remember as the most painful experiences I'd ever had to endure. The first was when I was with Nicholas, being ineffectively cleansed of my mating bond. The second was the emotional pain of losing Raif on the altar. The third, which was by far the most painful, was when I became complete.

I'd cocooned myself in Stephan's room for three days, only leaving the makeshift comfort of his bed to use the bathroom. I couldn't eat, and he didn't force me to. He stayed glued to my side every minute of the day. I couldn't have cared less. He could've left me alone with Nicholas's tender mercies, and I wouldn't have cared. I understood in those three days why mates died together. I craved death, an end to my suffering. I had nothing to hold me to this earth. A vast emptiness engulfed my very soul.

When I slept, I had nightmares of Raif. I'd be running in the Everglades, desperately trying to find him. Yet each time I did, he was a cold, lifeless shell of a man. Each time, I woke screaming in pain.

By the evening of the third day, the heart-wrenching loneliness and despair had dissipated into nothing. I was numb. I knew this was better than the pain but couldn't bring myself to care. I couldn't laugh, or cry, or feel anger. I was a hollow core of nothingness. I almost preferred the debilitating depression to the emptiness. I felt like my heart had gone to the void and was simply waiting for my body to join it. Stephan noticed the change in me and closed the club.

"Tasha," he whispered against my cheek. "*Miña mascota*, please be strong. The healers are here, as am I. Please don't leave me."

I'm not sure he meant to say the last, but it made the numbness bearable. My brain recognized his closing of the club as important. He never closed. It was a safe house above all else, a sanctuary for those who needed it. Closing the club was eliminating the only haven in this state. I didn't care.

I curled up into a ball on Stephan's bed, comfortable in my cocoon of emptiness. Dozing off to the silence of the club that matched the silence inside me, I was as content as I could be while Stephan sat in one of his chairs, watching over me. I wasn't peaceful or disturbed; I simply existed.

Out of nowhere, the pain ripped through my heart, expanding to touch every cell in my body. A scream escaped as my body contracted in on itself. Sweat poured from me as I writhed in agony. I gagged on blood. My spine bowed until my feet touched my scalp, and I continued to scream. The pain was unlike anything I'd ever felt before.

Blood curdling screams of pain and terror ripped from my throat. I was burning from the inside out as someone sliced me to bits, yet I was completely alone in Stephan's bed. Stephan stood by, helpless as the transformation took me. The healers looked on from the doorway, none truly knowing what to do.

My vision turned a pink-tinted, watery blur as my eyes cried blood. What had started out as sweat quickly turned into blood seeping through my pores. I couldn't think or feel anything past the agonizing pain. His sheets were soaked with my essence. My screams were long and loud, barely stopping as I took a breath. They ended abruptly with a final beat of my heart.

Stephan was holding me immediately. He was talking nonsense, encouraging me to stay, to fight. His voice broke as he pleaded with me, begging me to hold on. For him.

His tears were hot on my frozen skin. His whole body was a furnace next to mine. I blinked in confusion as my body started to tremble violently. Stephan must have seen something in my eyes signaling that the end of my suffering was near.

"Praise Poseidon!" he whispered as he clutched me tightly against his burning chest. Effortlessly, he carried me to the bathroom. Two women I didn't know filled the large tub with steaming water. Carefully, he stepped into the hot water, still clutching me in a tight embrace. His arms were the only things holding me together. My body thrashed as I shivered.

The hot water burned every inch of my skin as he sat down. I groaned in pain, tears leaking from my eyes for the first time since I'd mated.

"Shh, Tasha, it's okay. You have to get warm, get your blood flowing again. You should be fine in a moment. You're safe now. It's over." The relief in his voice was palpable. Tears of joy spilled down his cheeks as he smiled at me.

The trembling slowly subsided, and I relaxed in his arms, exhaustion claiming me in its sweet embrace. I found myself in and out of consciousness for a long time.

I'd been returned to my room, the familiar scents a balm on my psyche. I hid there for another week, alternating from nightmares to adjusting to the strange new things I was feeling from my body. Underneath it all was rage.

I thought I'd find peace with the change, but the only thing that was a constant throughout the days following Raif's death was a seething anger. I held onto it, letting it ground me as no emotion ever had before, knowing I'd need it to live through the wretched nightmares I couldn't escape.

My heart was thudding in my chest as I ran. I couldn't remember if I was running toward something or away. Fear ate away at my gut, but I couldn't recall why I was so afraid. The first hot stab of pain lanced through my torso, causing my steps to falter, reminding me what was happening.

No! *I thought, desperation causing my stride to move faster than my cheetah's body should ever go. I was so close; if I could just get there in time, I could save him. The brief reminder that Raif was in danger, hurt, and probably dying, pushed me further into my frenzied state. Branches tore at my skin as I ran through the trees. I could feel blood streaming down my pelt.*

My muscles started to seize as the clearing came into view. I changed faster than I ever had before, my cat form sliding away like shed clothing. I didn't care that I was bleeding and naked. All that mattered was the broken man in front of me. My stride faltered briefly at the sight of the wounds on his chest. He had to be alive. I didn't know how he could be, but he had to be.

I flew to his side, gathering him into my arms to protect him from further harm. His body offered no resistance to my touch. He was pale, blood oozing from the many stab wounds he'd sustained. I brushed his hair from his face, pleading for him to wake.

"Raif. Raif! Please, wake up! Please, dear God, wake up!" I screamed my agony to the heavens, closing my eyes against the truth in my arms. "Raif, Please! Amada, *wake up, wake up!" I felt strong arms shaking me. I made it! He would live! I pulled him closer. The relief I felt was palpable. I felt wetness on my lips, and I licked it off, thinking his tears were sweeter than I remembered.*

The next moment, he was lying on top of me. His hard body pressed almost uncomfortably against my curves. I started licking his wounds closed, purrs wracking my body as I licked. He shuddered. His legs pressed harder against my body, searching for a way to release some pressure. I opened for him. His erection ground hotly against my core, and I writhed in delight. He groaned.

I licked his chest again, savoring the sweet, coppery taste of his blood. He moaned, thrusting helplessly against me. I would've helped free him from the confines of his blasted pants, but my hands were held immobile above my head. My eyes had long been glued shut from the sweat and blood that covered my body. Something that should've had me paralyzed in horror made no difference to me with the realization that Raif was still alive. The only way I could comfort and entice him was with my tongue. I continued to clean his wounds, each lick being rewarded with a sweet taste of his essence and a heartfelt groan.

"Tasha, please. You have to stop. I'm still just a man. Please, for the love of Poseidon, stop." A voice groaned, pained words barely registering in my euphoric mind. I realized he'd been begging for a while now. I stopped purring and licking to listen.

"Tasha, please wake up. For the love of Poseidon, please stop and wake up." He groaned again, trying desperately to restrain the passion I was inadvertently invoking in him. The only thing that registered in my sleep-filled mind was that Raif had never called me Tasha.

My eyes flew open. Stephan's bloody chest was inches from my face. The lines of his body were taught with restraint. He was valiantly trying to hold me down and contain his lust at the same time. He felt me stiffen beneath him. His molten silver eyes met mine, the passion causing them to swirl.

"You can let me go now," I whispered. "What happened?"

He kept his gaze focused on mine. He watched me as if he were afraid of what I was going to do next. He leaned back slowly, releasing his hold on my arms and sitting on his heels in the cradle of my thighs.

"Oh my God! Stephan, did I do that?" His torso had long scratches dug into it as if an animal had attacked him. Most of them were licked clean, the healing properties in his blood and my saliva already leaving behind red healing tissue to mar his perfect skin. In another hour, they'd be completely gone, but some of the scratches were so bad that even with our natural healing properties, blood still oozed slowly from them. I reached for his chest to gauge the finger span. It matched mine perfectly. He shuddered at my touch.

"I was forced to restrain you, or you would have killed me. You are certain you are well now?" He was still trembling.

"I'm so sorry, Stephan. I didn't know. Are you okay?" I looked at him, the horror of what I'd done evident on my face.

"I will survive. I must go to feed now, but I need to know that you will be well." He was returning to his formal speak, and I knew things were bad.

"I'm fine, Stephan. I didn't mean to hurt you. This was my fault. Please, let me help you now." I turned my chin and threw my hair back over my shoulder, baring my neck for his use.

"For the love of Poseidon! My control is sorely lacking tonight as it is. I would not be able to control myself." He moved to leave, and I sprang up, shoving my wrist into his face.

"My blood is the strongest you'll find! You want it. I want you to take it. Drink!" I knew what I was asking of him. I felt horrible. Yes, his bite was orgasmic, but that was a by-product of his feeding. It didn't mean anything. He needed to heal, and it was my fault he was injured. I could deal with the effects of his bite if it meant I could help him.

With the vein so close and his hunger so strong, he couldn't resist. I shuddered in anticipation as he grabbed my arm, his mouth latching hungrily onto my wrist. He moaned as my blood hit his tongue just as I bit my lip to suppress the moan I wanted to release.

We climaxed together, still separated by the thin barrier of our clothes. He licked at the small puncture wounds longer than was necessary, gently massaging the tender tissue.

"Thank you," he whispered just before he fled the room.

I fell to the floor in a graceless heap. I waited until I heard the door's faint click before I collapsed. Hot, wet, salty tears streamed helplessly down my cheeks, a further reminder of what I'd lost and how different I truly was. The nightmare had been one of many that'd been plaguing my dreams since Raif's death.

However, this had been the first time I'd attacked someone. The reminder of Raif's death compounded with the knowledge that I'd hurt Stephan so much caused me unbearable pain. The two men

I loved more deeply than anything in this world were taken from me by fate's cruelty. The hurt, anger, and bitterness I felt poured from my body in gut-wrenching sobs.

I curled into a ball on my side, my back facing the door, desperately trying to pull myself together. The tears I'd missed so badly were now more of an annoyance, a weakness I no longer wanted. I cursed Poseidon, the fates, and anyone else I could blame.

I cursed Raif for not telling me of the whole prophecy and then leaving me. I cursed Stephan for allowing me to fall in love with him. We could never be together—neither of us would merge with another again after the loss of our mates. Finally, I cursed myself for my foolishness. Only I could be so naïve as to believe that a soul mate would be the end of my perpetual loneliness. There were never any guarantees in life, happiness being top on that list.

I cried for all the loss in my life. I released all the pain with the tears that streamed down my face and onto the marble tile that was so cold against my overly heated body. I stayed on the cold marble floor, weeping for everything I'd ever wanted in life and would never have. I hadn't cried since the night Raif died and didn't realize how desperately I needed the release. I cried so hard my muscles stiffened. I was finally at the end of my tears when I felt a pair of strong arms scoop me up.

Stephan lifted me from the floor and carried me to the fluffy canopy bed he'd picked out for me. I clung to him as tightly as I could, not willing to let him go. He winced slightly. I'd forgotten that I was stronger now, even as emotionally depleted as I was. He murmured some nonsensical words, and I loosened my grip. He set me down, intending to leave as soon as I was covered. I pulled him in next to me, needing his comfort more than I cared about propriety. He curled in next to me, and I finally relaxed. Clutching me close to his chest, he rubbed my back in slow, random circles.

I was content for the first time in a very long time. We both fell into a much-needed sleep, pretending for just a moment that we were allowed to be together.

18

A week went by, and while I still had nightmares, I hadn't attacked anyone since. Stephan returned to his room and his duties, leaving me to do what I wanted in the club. I was weak, my body still recuperating from the massive change it had gone through. Neither one of us knew what I'd be capable of once I fully recovered, but Stephan promised to help me learn control.

He and I were now the two most powerful beings on the planet. It was strange to think of myself in that light, especially since I could barely function. Remembering Stephan's story about his change, I had a deep-seated respect for him. I couldn't fathom fighting in my current state. His rage must have been a truly terrible thing for him to be able to withstand this transformation alone.

With lightness to my steps, I bathed, dressed, and went downstairs for breakfast. I was finally capable of starting my new life, to see what the future held. I was smiling as I walked into the small kitchen behind the bar. This place was filled with hidden hallways and rooms. It amazed me that the general public never became aware of any of the things going on behind the dance floor. I inhaled deeply as I walked into the kitchen. John was making cupcakes.

"Natasha! I'm so glad to see you up and about. How are you? You look wonderful." He gave me a big hug as I came around the counter. I sat on a stool to lick the chocolate off the spatula.

"I'm okay," I replied tentatively, smiling with the realization that it was true. I was okay. I was healing. "I'm starving. Do you have any breakfast left?" He laughed.

"I love having a Changer in the house. One breakfast coming up!" Grinning and chatting about nonsense, he started making a feast.

We hung out in the kitchen as I ate, and he continued to bake. John loved to cook. It was his not-so-secret pastime, and he excelled at it. He typically made all the meals for the non-vampires of the house, but as those were few and far between, he hadn't practiced his calling as often as he'd like until I came. I loved to eat. We made a great pair. Casually, I brought up a subject that'd been previously avoided.

"I was thinking about going to the house today. Do you think Stephan could spare you for a few hours to go with me?"

John paled at my question. Neither of us had left the sanctuary of the club without vampiric supervision since we'd been abducted. John still sported a wicked scar on his chest from what his brother had done to him. I needed to know that the place I loved, the place I wanted to call home, was still safe. I had to show him he'd be safe there too, because I was hoping he'd come with me.

"Are you sure you're ready for that?" he whispered.

"It's my home. I need to know that it's safe. Come with me?"

I had a special bond with John, whether he felt it or not. He was mine, my human to protect and care for. I wasn't sure when or how it had happened, but I knew without a doubt that John belonged to me. I felt strange having proprietary feelings toward him but knew they didn't extend further than that. It was a bond I'd never felt before. He was mine, and I would protect any family he chose to have. I hid my smile as he sighed, knowing he'd come with me so we could face our fears together.

"Stephan's not going to like this."

An hour later, I was learning just how right John was. Stephan paced his office as he yelled at me.

"No." His tone was fierce. "Absolutely not. You're not ready."

"I'll be fine," I said, but he wasn't listening.

"You have no idea what your new abilities are. What happens if you call the earth and swallow John in the yard?" A smirk curled on my lips as he started cursing at me in Atlantean. He only did that when I'd really ticked him off, and I found it hilarious.

"Come with us then," I interjected as he paused to catch his breath.

"You know I can't do that right now. Victoria's still missing, and the Werewolves are still upset about the twin's death." I winced at that, knowing both issues were my fault.

Victoria saw me curled in Stephan's arms after Raif died. She left Stephan's kiss, going rogue, the night I became whole. The only thing Stephan and I could figure was that she'd listened to his heart-wrenching pleas for me to return to him. She'd expressed infatuation to Stephan on more than one occasion, and I guessed that hearing him profess his love for another was more than she could take. We hadn't heard from her since, and Stephan was a mess.

He'd claimed her just as I'd claimed John. His feelings toward her never extended past protector and mentor. She was his responsibility; one he cared deeply for. He took his role seriously, never truly understanding the depth of the feelings she had for him.

The twins he referred to were Tommy and Ben. They weren't part of Nicholas's clan, but hired help from the Werewolf clan. Autochthon, Auto as he was called now, was their leader and was angry with Stephan for killing them. Stephan was trying to keep my involvement out of it and spread the news that Nicholas and his clan were destroyed in a turf war.

It was apparently something that happened every so often, so it wouldn't come as any surprise. Those that were killed that weren't part of the clan were supposed to be returned to their home clans to be disposed of by the respective clan leader. As there wasn't anything left of the bodies, Stephan couldn't return them to Auto. He now owed Auto compensation, but Stephan was resisting, feeling it wasn't justified because of what the twins had done to me. As he wasn't willing to divulge that information to anyone outside those that already knew, it was causing frustration between the two alphas.

It was a gigantic mess; one I thought could be easily resolved if Stephan just told Auto what happened. The Werewolf clan wasn't known to look kindly toward torture. Stephan kept telling me he wanted to protect me from having to continue to relive that pain.

"I have to go back to the house, Stephan," I whispered, pleading with him to hear what I couldn't say. I had to go back to that house and face my fears, know that I was safe and could protect myself. I had to know it was over.

He looked at me then, really looked at me, not through me like he'd been doing lately. Slowly, he nodded. I gave him a timid smile. I knew eventually I'd have to go back to Nicholas's compound, to see for myself that it really was destroyed, but I wasn't ready for that. My wounds still needed more time to heal. Visiting my house was a step in that direction. He grabbed my hand as I turned to go. His voice was tight with fear as he spoke.

"Please be careful. I don't know what I'd do if I lost you again." He placed his other hand on my cheek, moving to run his fingers through my hair. I smiled at him, fighting the attraction that threatened to break through the pain I still felt.

"I'll be back by nightfall," I said, impulsively kissing him goodbye. His lips were moist and soft. I pulled away before it went any further, blood boiling with passion in my veins.

John and I arrived at the house almost an hour later, pale and trembling. I looked over at him and tried to appear encouraging and strong.

"You don't have to do this, you know. No one would blame you for being uneasy here and never wanting to come back." John tried one last time to convince me to abandon my quest. He only succeeded in strengthening my resolve.

"I would," I said, climbing out of the car before my nerves could change my mind.

The house was spectacular in the late afternoon sun. The workers had finished everything I'd asked, and I knew the furniture was inside. I closed my eyes, breathing in the warm, moist air and listening to the sounds around me. I could smell the fragrant flowers John and I had planted over the scents of pine and grass. The musky, thick scent of pond water blended with chemicals to kill mosquitos tantalized my nose, reminding me of when I'd played here with Stephan. The birds called, frogs croaked, and crickets started singing their songs.

I found the peaceful serenity I'd remembered.

I heard John's door open and felt a small smile tug at my lips. I walked into the house, my steps renewed with the peaceful existence of the Everglades. John sighed behind me, running to catch up. I could feel nervous waves of energy radiating off him, but he was trying to be as strong as me. I winked at him, enjoying the confused look he gave me.

The house sparkled under the glow of the electric lighting. I breathed a sigh of relief. I was home.

JEAN BOOTH

Author's Note

When I first decided I would write a book about supernatural beings, *Changed* was closer to what I had in mind than *Choice*. I never intended to write something nearly as erotic as Choice. I wanted action, adventure, and mystery. What Natasha had in mind for me was something entirely different, and I'm glad it came out like it did.

There are so many people who helped me get to this point, and without them, I'd have given up and gone back to nursing, where my life was stressful, annoying, and safe. To those who've encouraged me, and continue to ask for the next installment, thank you. You have no idea what your kind words do to soothe the soul.

For my dad and step-mom, your support means the world to me, and one of these days, I'll write a story Dad won't get creeped out by. Bryan, you mean the world to me, and I thank you for giving me the space and time I need to write, even if you don't understand why I like it so much.

Always, and most importantly, thank you to my fans—without your support and encouragement I wouldn't be here. You guys rock!

Last, thanks to my editor, Abi. You are able to get into the insanity that is my head and help clarify what I'm trying to say. I both love and hate you, but mostly love. A relationship between editor and author is complex, and I hope ours lasts for a long time. Thanks for all you do.

I hope you enjoyed this installment of the Origin series. Origin Shorts, *Created*, *Consumed*, and *Convergence* are next. I never intended to write from anyone's perspective besides Natasha, but Victoria's story begged to be told. That, and the shorts were never intended to be part of this series, but without them, this it wouldn't be nearly as amazingly fun as it is. Convergence is kicking my tail—so many voices, so many things happening, not sure what to focus on first. We'll get there, and Atlantis is sure to bring some excitement once she breaches the surface.

Thank you.
~Jean

ABOUT THE AUTHOR

JEAN BOOTH was born in Las Vegas, Nevada on a sweltering summer night. She's traveled to many states, living in Michigan, Minnesota, Florida, Nevada, and Maryland. She, along with those that know her, affectionately refer to her as "The Crazy Cat Lady." She's worked in healthcare and done grant management for the entirety of her adult life and was challenged in 2010 to finally start writing the stories that live in her head. She specializes in the Paranormal.

When not writing, Jean enjoys cruising on the back of her motorcycle, or reading everything and anything fiction. She's also considered to be extremely "crafty", making everything from clothing to jewelry to painting.

To find out more about Origins and to see what's coming soon visit jeanbooth.com.